BLAZING GLORY: TRICK OR TREAT?

Dedication

"Let the little children come to me. Don't stop them, because the kingdom of God belongs to people who are like these children. I tell you the truth, you must accept the kingdom of God as if you were a child, or you will never enter it."

Luke chapter 18 verses 16 & 17

Blazing Glory is dedicated to all boys and girls who are yet to find Jesus Christ as their friend and Saviour.

Blazing Glory

Trick or Treat?

KAREN DAVIES

Illustrated by David Colbourne

CROSSED OVER

First published 2008

Published by Crossed Over
www.crossed-over.org

ISBN: 978 0 9559463 0 1

Illustrations by David Colbourne
Edited by Anna Leggett

Book design and production for the publisher by
Bookprint Creative Services, <www.bookprint.co.uk>
Printed in Great Britain.

Contents

Symbols in *Trick or Treat?*

As you read the story you will discover eight powerful symbols. Use them as keys to unlock the amazing mysteries that are hidden between the pages of this book.

 1. When you see the binoculars, it's time to stop and look up important messages in your Bible. Open your Bible at the place shown and read what Father God has to say. (See "The Bookworm's Guide to the Bible" on page 9 to find out how to navigate your way around the Bible.)

 2. Treasure the compass and turn it to follow the characters towards Blazing Glory. Discover the hidden path you must follow to the way, the truth and the life.

 3. Some situations don't change instantly but a little time is needed before you unlock the miracle that is

waiting for you. Even if the world around you seems to be spinning around in chaos like a whirlwind, you can wait and stay safe in the eye of peace.

4. The feather is a very important symbol and is only given to those who are good listeners. It points you to special words in the Bible. As you read these words, hear the gentle voice of Father God speaking especially to you. (See "The Bookworm's Guide to the Bible" on page 9 to help you find the Bible passages.)

5. Whenever you see this symbol, pray to Jesus along with the characters in the story. To pray just means to talk to Jesus, as you would talk to your best friend. Your prayers will unlock the help that you need.

6. This symbol represents the Eternal Fruit Garden. Enter into the garden and taste the fruit of living words that will change who you are and what you thought you knew. You will also collect twelve eternal fruit badges as you follow Father God's instructions.

7. The heart symbol opens the door to the Hideaway. In this special quiet place you can enjoy personal friendship times with Father God. He only shares his mysteries and secrets with his friends.

8. Each jewel is rewarded when an important lesson is learnt. It will be stored up as treasure that will be invested in order to unlock the final prize in Blazing Glory.

The Bookworm's Guide to the Bible – The Living Manual

Hey, here's a little guidance so you can wriggle your way through the pages of your exciting Bible. Follow these simple steps and dig away. When you see the and symbols in the story, here's what to do:

↘ The Bible is made up of 66 books. There are 39 in the Old Testament and 27 in the New Testament.
↙ Look at the Contents page in your *Blazing Glory Bible* and find the page number the book is found on and turn to that page.
↖ Every book has chapters.
↗ The next step is to find the correct chapter number. It's the largest number on the page.
↙ When you have found the right book and correct chapter you are just seconds away from the verse.

↙ The verses are numbered in every chapter, with little numbers right next to the words you are to read.

For your first dig, why not look up and read 2 Timothy chapter 3 verse 16. If you can't find it, don't worry. Why not ask someone who can show you how to find it? Think about what it says here – how Father God, the author of the Bible, inspired men to write down what he wanted to say to his people. The Bible is God's living message to the world.

Character Photo Gallery

Devine

Vermont

Prince Beelzebub

THE GLIDES

THE DUPES

THE STALKERS

Bully Bear

Cyril

Wiz

THE STALKERS

1

Fowl Swoop

If you are reading this book then you are probably quite clever. And if you are quite clever then you probably think that you know quite a lot. But let me warn you, this book is very powerful, especially in the right hands. Maybe the right hands could be your hands? Proceed with caution as this will blow the cover off what you thought you knew. Hold tight to the book and when you get to the end you will find a new beginning. Once upon a day, there comes a time when you are given the chance to take a fantastic flight of discovery into a true and lasting friendship. That day has arrived.

Our ordinary feathered friends were each faced with this very same choice. Which group were they to join and which path were they to follow as they made their swift fowl swoop to the Camp of Life? Having spent their early chirpy days in the comforts of their home nest, these six birds had applied to the Camp of Life Academy, to spend time away from their familiar safety nest. Each bird was eager to face the challenge to follow their heart in preparation for a life with the high flyers. The following weeks would determine their flight path. Would it be upwards towards Blazing Glory or would they crash land and remain grounded having followed the crowd on the path of tricks and treats?

It was the first day for the new intake at the Camp of Life. The sun beamed brightly across the clear blue sky, welcoming the students. One by one, each bird would make its fowl swoop into the academy. They were to be greeted by the Master. He would be in charge of our young fledglings. With eyes sharp and piercing, burning with the fire of Blazing Glory, the Master waited expectantly for the chosen few.

The first to be tossed from his family nest to make his journey to the Camp of Life was Oscar the young eagle. Soaring high on the thermals, he thought he would spend some eagle time alone and ride high above the campsite. As a learned bird, a high flyer for his age, Oscar decided that it would be wise to explore how the land lay and discover some of its secret sites. Oscar soared like a champion, alone and yet supported by the safe and strong currents swirling around the skies. He wanted to be the first to catch a glimpse of Blazing Glory itself. All Oscar had ever heard about it was that it was a mysterious place, bright and beautiful beyond all our imagination.

Meanwhile, Melody the songbird had been tossed from the great height of her family nest. Their nest had become overcrowded since the new arrival of her baby brother. Melody was unusually young to attend the Camp of Life, however, it was her mother's only option. Melody knew about the stories of Blazing Glory, and from an early age longed to discover more of this enduring, everlasting city. Despite this amazing adventure on the horizon, Melody felt a little sad. Blinking back the tears at leaving her family behind, Melody swallowed hard and did the only thing she knew how to do: she burst into the song "All things bright and beautiful", her favourite school hymn. What started as a harmonic song of praise soon became a squawking cry as she quickly remembered her fear of heights! Melody made it as far as the words 'all creatures great and small' and then began plummeting rapidly to the ground.

Towering above, Oscar was still enjoying his exploration of the campsite when his sharp eyes caught a glimpse of Melody's distressing fall.

Following his heroic heart, in a dramatic swoop he quickly descended beneath Melody to catch her seconds before she hit the ground. With his chest pounding, he delivered her safely to the feet of their Master. With a searching look at the trembling pair, the Master softly breathed, "There is no greater love than to lay down your own life for your friends."

🔭 John chapter 15 verse 13

Classes had not yet begun but the Master knew that Oscar had already learned a lesson which would enable them to make it to their destination. This was possibly one of the greatest lessons of all: the need to help each other in a selfless way. It was at this point that Melody and Oscar knew that they would be birds of a feather and would stick together throughout the journey to Blazing Glory.

It wasn't long before trouble plunged from the skies: Jack the jackdaw. As soon as he had flown his family nest he became distracted with the things that glitter but are not gold. Jack made many stops on his way to camp, swiftly poking his sharp beak into several nests, taking what did not belong to him. Stealing from others, he took a swift flight off with the booty. Jack stuffed his flight bag with lots of shiny paper and pearls. Soon his flight bag became overweight and he landed at camp with a loud thud.

"Anything to declare?" demanded the Master.

Trying to hide his stolen goods and to distract the others, Jack chirped, "I declare, who are these two feathered specimens?" turning all attention onto Oscar and Melody.

Stepping forward with his chest pushed high, Oscar proudly announced himself, "Oscar the overcomer."

Appearing from beneath Oscar's enormous wings the small songbird piped up, "I'm Melody. Watch me climb the height of any scale!"

"As long as you don't look down," muffled Oscar under his feathers.

At that moment, with feathers ruffled, who should bomb through the clouds but Charlie the parrot. Charlie was notorious for repeating everything he heard, and for adding his own extra bit of colour to the tale. He soon made his presence known.

"What's all this extra baggage here then? Featherweight for the journey, that's what I was told," he pointed out with his sharp beak.

Just to make matters worse he repeated this accusation over and over again. This was noted sadly by the Master. Seeing the Master's displeased look, Charlie slowly cowered behind Jack, hoping his annoying comments would be forgotten. Charlie then stumbled on the straps of Jack's flight bag. As he tripped, Charlie caught sight of the stolen goods hidden within the bag. Noticing Charlie's discovery, quick-thinking Jack charmed him with a promise to share the loot on the adventure.

"Keep quiet and stick with me mate," he said, "and half of this is yours."

So with tempting tales and flaps of his wings Jack had made for himself a gullible target in Charlie and found a way to keep his feathered friend's feet snared to the ground, safely by his side.

"What is this dazzling colour of frivolous feathers wafting to the ground?" choked Charlie on his beak. "Wafting to the ground," he repeated, as he gazed at the new chick, Delilah, arriving at camp. "Why, why, why Delilah, don't you come and nestle over here with Jack and me?" twittered Charlie.

Delilah was a little late as it had taken her so long to pack the latest fashion feathers with the most up-to-date colours. Delilah took a glance at Melody and Oscar but upon noticing Jack's designer bag, was quickly enticed by the invitation to join the boys.

"Hmm," sighed Delilah, as she reapplied the lip gloss to her beak. Glad I used my best perfume today as I did not realize how many would be in my captive audience," she thought. "I hope they notice my beautiful feathers," mused Delilah, brushing them neatly into place.

Delilah picked up a piece of Jack's shiny silver paper to catch a glimpse of her reflection. She tilted her head back and poised her beak into her favourite film star pose. Delilah had become so busy attending to herself that she missed the unfortunate descent of our final but not so pretty feathered friend, Penny the sparrow.

Penny the sparrow had spent much of her short life moving from nest to nest with her grandmother, a lovely old sparrow. Penny's grandmother was frail and so the nests that she had built were often destroyed by the blustery winds. Although they were poor, Penny was always comforted in her grandmother's safe wings. Her grey feathers were just a mark of her great wisdom as she had cared solely for Penny. Her grandmother knew that the greatest gift that she could leave her little Penny was the chance to go to the Camp of Life. It was here that she knew Penny would be loved for who she was and guided on the way to Blazing Glory under the watchful care of the Master. On the way to camp, and with nothing but the feathers on her back, Penny had lost her way and had ended up in the gutter. Injured with a fractured wing, she made a very discreet and unnoticed entrance. However, nothing missed the keen attention of the Master. He gently placed his loving arm around her and guided her to Oscar and Melody whom he knew would become her trusted friends.

Today's chosen few were all present and correct: Oscar the eagle, Melody the songbird, Jack the jackdaw, Charlie the parrot, Delilah the chick and, last but not least, little Penny the young sparrow.

The night was beginning to draw in and there was a slight chill in the air. Noticing that Penny had started to shiver, the Master led the birds to a burning bush. Here, around the bush, they could feel safe in the light and sense the warmth of their Master's kindness towards them. Realizing that this was a special place, they shook the dust from their claws. Here they found rest and received instructions for their special quest. In the flickering light, something caught the attention of Oscar. As he looked closer at the Master he noticed what appeared to be some deep scars. With an inquisitive brow he stared at the marks, wondering how the Master had become wounded in this way. Little Penny had noticed them too. Feeling upset and alone, she moved in close to the Master and chirped out, "What are those holes in your hands and feet?" The Master gently picked up Penny with his loving hand. Melody hopped onto his hand too and, noticing the scars on his head, she flew up onto his shoulder and reached up carefully to stroke the wounds. A tear rolled from her tiny eye and splashed into the sizzling flames of the camp-fire.

With the strength of his love clearly marked on his body, the Master did not talk about the pain that had caused the

scars. The Master knew that each bird would have their own special time to discover on the journey how his great love had left a mark on history forever. He just spread out his arms to shadow them in his care and talked to them as his friends.

With great love and detail the Master began to tell them about Blazing Glory, the homeland where his Father God lived, also called Heaven. The Master had come to guide them there, as he was the only way to Blazing Glory. He had been sent to earth by his Father, the ruler of this blazing, glorious kingdom. The Master was his only Son. At the beginning of time, the whole of Creation had fallen to the ground and chosen its own way to go, losing its way to Blazing Glory. The

Master had come to lift everyone out of the mud of their wrongdoing – which is also called sin – making them free to spend the rest of their lives flying and following the right way to Blazing Glory. One day they would go to this wonderful home to live with their Father forever.

The Master told them how he had laid his life down for the world so that everyone could know his Father as a personal friend. He spoke with such strength in the tone of his voice that it made their feathers stand up on end.

"Now is the day, and today is the time to choose my way, so that you can live free from the mud of sin. Do not be trapped by the angry fowler," he told them. The young birds pressed in closer. The Master continued, looking at each of them in turn, "He secretly flies from his tomb of darkness and wants to mess your life up and keep you in the mud. He is an evil genius, with tricks and treats. Be careful, he has come to rob you from being truly free to fly to Blazing Glory." The Master then smiled as he explained, "Your quest and adventure start around this camp-fire. Here you will see that I have come so that you can have true life, a life that doesn't end here."

He looked upwards and after a short pause whispered, "This is just the beginning of a forever flight into Blazing Glory, prepared for those who love and follow me. If you love me you will obey what I ask you to do."

"Obey, obey?" repeated Charlie. "That doesn't sound like living to me. What do you think, Chick?"

"Are fancy feathers part of your flight package? Are you sure what you say is for real?" enquired Delilah.

The Master turned and looked at the three little rascals – Jack, Charlie and Delilah – with a piercing gaze that ruffled their feathers. They stepped back into the shadows, away from the heart-searching gaze of the Master.

The Master pulled out from behind him six bright bags for each of the students. He lovingly handed each bird their own personal flight bag and said, "Here's your flight bag for a lifetime of adventure. In it you will find my Father's manual for life. It's called the Bible. Every word in it written down by a feather quill pen was directed by him. He spoke the living words to those who listened to him and they wrote down his detailed instructions. Every word carries his breath and will give you the power to live in the way he wants you to."

Penny looked into her bag and found her Bible. "My very own Bible, chirpy, chirpy, cheep, cheep." She squealed with joy and delight as she had no personal belongings, not even a bag to speak of. Now she was the proud owner of the greatest gift ever given and she decided she would treasure it forever.

"Do what it says?" repeated Charlie. "How do you expect us to know what to do with this? How will we ever fly lugging this bag around?"

Patiently listening, the Master showed his understanding nature towards Charlie. It was for little ones like Charlie that the Master had suffered to make the journey to Blazing Glory possible. Even though the invitation wasn't deserved, the opportunity was there for whoever would follow the way. The Master kindly answered, "As you read your Bible, the words will go deep into your heart so that you can make the right choices, even when you can't see the way through. As you fly in the direction it guides you to go, it will be like a bright lamp to your feet and headlights shining ahead."

"Wow!" responded Oscar with great anticipation. "I can't wait to fly as high as I can."

"High, who said high?" shrilled Melody, whose fear of heights grounded any thoughts of hope.

Jack found something nice and shiny in his bag and, pecking at the glittering metal frantically, asked, "What's this special treasure?"

With pointed clear words the Master explained, "That's your very own compass. It points to the way, the truth and the life. This always shows the way to the Father, directed by the truth of his words." The Master glanced at the ground and sighed. "I have left a special path to help you – this is the way which you should follow. It's not an easy trail," he said. Then looking upwards he smiled, "But I have gone ahead of you, making sure the way is safe. There may be times when you feel you are lost. What you must do is look carefully and I will dust the highway with clean white snow so that you will know the course you must follow. Now I have to go back to Blazing Glory to get everything ready for all who choose it as their forever home."

Penny moved in close, as she felt unsure and said, "Please don't go away. Everyone close to me has gone away and I feel so snug and safe here with you."

With strength and confidence the Master reassured little Penny and the others, who were hiding their fears. "Don't be troubled, because you will feel my presence in another way when the Father sends you a special helper. He will stick around; so closely, in fact, that he will be like a loyal brother. Don't worry, he will guarantee your place in Blazing Glory as you become part of our great family. He will come and show you the way and will teach you the truth. He is strong, white and pure, and as gentle as a dove. Follow his guidance and let him be your strength. You can't make it alone; you need him and each other."

As he finished speaking, happiness filled the air and the feathered fowl broke into a playful pillow fight. This was started by Charlie of course, who had accused the others of taking an extra helping of red berries at supper. With a red-stained beak, Jack looked guilty of the charge. He licked his beak quickly to hide the evidence. Suddenly, a pillow broke and all the feathers flew into the air, drifting slowly to the ground like a blanket of snow.

With a feather resting on his lip the Master coughed, "Children, I have got my eye on you. I never go to sleep, but it is time for you to rest and close your eyes. Tomorrow is a bright new day. Snuggle up and rest close to me. I'm going away soon, so look out for the helper in the morning. Remember, whenever you see the symbol of 🪶 a feather, know that your Father is taking care of you. Look up and read the given passage in the Bible and his gentle words will strengthen and encourage you as you find your way to Blazing Glory."

2
Flickering Flame

The flame flickered brightly against the backdrop of the dark night sky. The Master settled the young ones down to sleep. He left Oscar with a bottle of red berry juice and a loaf of bread for him to share with the others as they travelled together. This was to remind them of the Master on their journey. The Master explained carefully that the red drink and bread were for life and health but that they were only for those who receive his words.

Lying down to rest they began to count the stars and wonder about all the things they had been told. Little Penny felt small as she tried to grasp the thought that there was a Father in Blazing Glory who knew her name. Such love and care was too great for her small heart to contain, but this knowledge left her feeling warm on the inside. Their attention became fixed on one strange cloud that shone brightly in the sky. It seemed like a window had opened in the heavens. The Master then stretched out his powerful arms and was lifted high into the night air. His arms were like a canopy of love over his Father's Creation. The Master's final words rested like gentle dew around where they lay as he told them to watch for the blaze of glory in the skies, as he would return one day, in the same way he had left.

A gust of wind, like a swirl of peace, moved around the camp. A sense of peace had rested on the campsite and had increased as the Master left. One by one, each of the birds closed their eyes to sleep. Oscar was the last to close his watchful eye as he quite naturally had taken the lead in caring for the little ones, especially Penny and Melody who felt safe tucked under his wing.

Whilst they were sleeping and just before the light rays of the morning began to shine, a thick cloud of darkness tried to penetrate and disturb the peace that was keeping them safe. A swirl of wind lifted and scattered the surrounding twigs and leaves, and then an eerie, cold silence followed. Wakened by the cold air of the darkness, Oscar sensed the looming danger. He swiftly swooped Penny and Melody up onto his back and took flight so that they would be safe in the protection of peace left by the Master.

However, Charlie, Jack and Delilah decided that they wanted to see for themselves what this invasion of darkness was.

"It's harmless, it's harmless," repeated Charlie. He enjoyed mischief and trouble. From out of the shadows two enormous wings were raised into the sky as a gust of wind breezed through the camp with a terrifying chill. Trying to be brave but quivering with fright, Charlie, Jack and Delilah held each other's wings but were fixed to the ground with fear.

Vermont the vulture had landed and was an uninvited guest. He was a powerful creature of the night. Vermont was armed with powers from a dark place and terrified the shaking audience with sparks of magic from his bag of tricks. Vermont introduced himself as Captain of the Dupes. He told them tales of hidden mysteries and tried to entice them to

follow him into dark and fascinating places. Out of sight, Oscar was flying high above the darkness, with Melody and Penny clutching onto his safe wings. They were above any thoughts that would chase away the vapour of peace that held them out of the way of trouble. Oscar hoped the other birds would remember the Master's advice to check their manuals, looking to see if their compasses pointed the right way.

As if by magic, Vermont the vulture pulled out a bright sugary bag of tricks and treats to entice the soon-to-be-tormented trio. Jack, with sharp eyes, saw the shiny paper inside the bag and was hooked in an instant. Although not too sure, Charlie soon followed Jack's lead into Vermont's snare of treats. As for Delilah, well, she could not resist a bag that colourful and appealing. Bewitched by the contents of

Vermont's bag, the three were wrapped in the dark cloud of his wicked wings. Charlie, Jack and Delilah left the safety of the burning fire and disappeared into the cloak of wooded darkness.

Oscar was flying high with Melody and Penny fastened like glue to his back. They had been shielded from the horrible scene on the ground. Little Penny had kept her eyes tightly shut as she had been told by her caring grandmother to be careful what she watched. They were being kept safe in the 🌀 eye of peace.

Oscar landed softly back at the campsite, with his little passengers on board his back, onto the feathers left over from the earlier pillow fight. Remembering their flight bags, they scurried over to the bush to find out what they should do. Looking through the bird's-eye binoculars, they flicked through the pages of their manuals with the tips of their wings to read:

🔭 John chapter 10 verse 10

"Mmmm," sang Melody, piecing the puzzle together. "If Vermont was really our captain and guide, he would not have come like a thief would he? What are we to do? What will become of them? What will become of us?" she cried.

It was just before dawn when one helpful feather flurried to the ground, pointing them to some words in their Bibles which they read together:

🪶 John chapter 15 verse 26

The gentleness of the Father's words touched their fear, chasing it away with his love. As they waited for the morning song to start, they saw something flicker in the dimming light of the fire. In its flames they saw a pure white dove, shimmering, with not a single flaw in its feathers. He hovered and rested upon each of them, a little puzzled as to why the other three birds had not waited for him. He comforted those who had patiently remained waiting.

Then something quite unusual happened.

Each of the three friends was filled with an incredible joy. Oscar did a loop de la hoop. Penny just rolled her tongue with new words that she couldn't even understand and which caused her to lift off the ground in a 🕊 prayer. As for Melody, she began singing new songs – tunes which could only have been written in Blazing Glory itself. What a morning of mornings! Shadows of that dark night were chased away.

Finally their claws touched the ground and Devine the dove was able to introduce himself to the young seekers. Intrigued by his wings, Penny wanted to know what the twelve brightly coloured badges were on the tips of his wing feathers.

"These are the twelve fruits from Blazing Glory. These eternal fruit badges are awards which are recognized and highly valued when you get to Blazing Glory and will enable the Father to quickly identify you as one of his children. You will discover them in the 🧺 Eternal Fruit Garden, which you will find when you enter your own special 💚 Hideaway. You will have the opportunity to spend time in your 💚 Hideaway as you go on your quest. It is found in the secret place of your heart where the Father will speak his words to you. You will learn to recognize his voice. He will speak in a soft and gentle whisper. Listen very carefully to his words so that you do what he asks. Hear with your heart what he says so that you follow his words with loving actions in a caring way. As you obey what the Father says, showing others his ways, you will receive the eternal fruit badges," explained Devine.

"When you enter your ♡ Hideaway, nothing harmful can touch you there as it is like a strong fortress. No arrows of doubt fired against you can bring you down. It is important that you shut the door and wait until any danger has passed. Then lift up your voice in 🏺 prayer and go forward, pressing on towards all the good things your Father has planned for your life. I am Devine, your captain, the Captain of the Glides," he said, stretching out his strong white wings. "I will teach you to rise above the laws of nature so that you can see things which cannot be achieved naturally. Things which are not possible for you to do will become possible with my power. The flight path may be dangerous and difficult but look:

🔭 Philippians chapter 4 verse 13

You will be ready for and equal to anything as you are strengthened by the Master. The Master's name is Jesus. Everything is possible for those who know Jesus."

The birds gasped with excitement as they remembered the scars on the Master and realized they had been with Jesus. Speechless, they continued to listen to Devine, hanging on his every breathed word.

"Everything has been tried and tested by Jesus. He has been through everything that you will go through and so will be able to help you with anything. Only remember, everything you do and ask for must be in line with what

Jesus would want for you." Devine then pulled out from under his wing the most dazzling jewel they had ever seen. The bright light of the morning danced around this most beautiful stone. It looked priceless. They all wondered where Devine had found such a gem. "When you learn one of Jesus's important lessons, your character will shine like a jewel. When I see this happening in you, a jewel will be added to your treasure in Blazing Glory, ready for when you finally fly home. Where your heart is, there your treasure will be found. These gems don't come easy. They can cost everything but are worth more than anything. Never forget, everything you do for the Father will one day be rewarded," explained Devine as the jewel reflected in his bright blue eyes. "You will be my three 'Glides' on this quest. If you are ready, pick up your flight bag with your manual and compass in and let me guide the way. Don't be afraid – all you need to do is let me be in control of every situation you face, and you'll be safe to fly another day to places you never dreamed possible. Are you ready to glide? Are you ready to ride to new heights?" asked Devine, lifting his wings ready to take flight.

Whilst the others moved towards the clear path that was the runway out of the campsite, Penny noticed something left by the smouldering bush. Turning her head in a panic, she shrieked, "Wait a minute, wait for me," flapping her little brown wings in a fury. "It's just our friends have left their flight bags behind. How will they know the way?"

Devine responded sadly, "They have, for the moment, rejected the answers found in the words of life. They did not wait for me. Instead they took the tricks and treats that will cheat them out of the things that will last forever. We can only pray that there will be another day and opportunity when I can be found by them again."

Looking a little terrified, Melody was a bit unsure of being part of the adventure due to her fear of heights. Lovingly, Oscar turned and noticed her quivering feathers and said, "Jump up here, Melody. You must learn to overcome your fear." Then, with a gentle nudge from Devine, Oscar lowered his other wing and invited Penny to hop up too. So they all flew into the morning, ready to colour a new day.

3

Arrow of Truth

High in the crisp blue sky, Devine dove-tailed the young Glides, remaining close behind them ready to say, "This is the way you must go today."

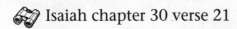 Isaiah chapter 30 verse 21

Penny watched, perched on Oscar's stately wing and wondered why Devine led from behind. She was soon to learn that he was her protection from any arrows that fly by night. Devine would remain their constant rearguard to keep them safe from any plot of trouble.

Oscar searched earnestly for the Blazing Glory trail, and with a feather of wisdom he plucked out his ⊕ compass from his flight bag. The arrow spun around and the magnet pointed towards the truth. The path below could not be seen because of all the dead wood that lay over its trail. Devine, aware of the difficulty, carried down fire in his wings to burn the dead wood out of the way, leaving the ashes to be blown by the wind of his visit. With the gentleness of his nature he then sprinkled the path with fresh clean white snow.

"Hey, what a day," said Oscar. "Who has ever seen fire and snow all in one breath?"

The feather of God's words tickled Melody into a song of praise as they landed on this snow-driven path to investigate the trail. Oscar hopped around as his claws made fresh marks on the crisp white snow. Penny jumped down with great excitement and rolled in the snow, ending up like a big snowball. Melody chuckled with delight and flew down to help brush down Penny's feathers as she shivered with cold.

On the horizon they could see a green hill. It seemed far away. They knew instinctively that the truth would be found there. Resting from their short journey together, Oscar took out of his bag the red berry juice and bread, which had been given to them at camp. As they took the bread in their beaks and drank the red berry juice, they understood how Jesus lived for truth. Flicking through their Bibles with their wing tips they quickly saw how Jesus never lied, sinned or fell to any trick of the evil genius. They read that Jesus lived for one purpose and that was completed on the green hill far away.

Aware of their discovery of truth, Devine quickly interrupted, knowing that this meant imminent danger. "I must warn you," he sharply pecked. "There were six applicants meant to be on this Blazing Glory trail today. Three have already been tricked out of the forever prize. The evil genius knew there were going to be six of you. He commissioned six cruel stalkers to try to bring you down and take you off course. They do not play by the rules and will use any nasty trick or treat they can find to lure you from the way."

Out of his bag, Devine took snapshots of the deadly characters the Glides were to watch out for. Feeling petrified, Penny trembled under Oscar's wing.

"There, there, my little friend, there's no need to be afraid of these bullies. Remember, Devine is at our rear and Jesus has already gone ahead so there is nothing to worry about," announced Oscar in a reassuring tone.

Coughing politely, Devine introduced the first deadly character. Holding up a photograph he said, "Meet Cyril the sulky snake. This miserable creature has been doomed to crawl in the dust of his lies and discouragement. Be very careful when you are on the ground. You must watch out for the poison on his tongue. His venom of lies and trickery can paralyze you with fear if you let his words touch you. Next . . ."

Penny interrupted, "Did you say nest? I don't like it here, it was much safer on the roof tops, out of harm's way. I need my grandmother. I need my nest." Penny continued to cry out uncontrollably.

Devine placed his pure white gentle wing on her tiny brown head and said, "No, Penny, remember you would only end up in the gutter if you went back to where you came from. Look how far you have come already. I'm so proud of you. Remember, I'm here to drive away any fear from your mind so that you stay free to fly to Blazing Glory."

Isaiah chapter 26 verse 3

"Next," repeated Devine, "meet Stavros the sly fox. He has a big red bushy tail that can dust you off course if you get close enough to listen to his lies. Stavros can be identified by the drips of saliva around his mouth. He always licks his lips in a tempting way when he is telling his tale of lies. Watch out and be shrewd because he's sly and old, practised in his tricks. Be warned, he loves to come out in the dark, so stay in the light of what the Father says."

Psalm 119 verse 105

"Memorize this verse. You are going to need it. Use it like a torch," taught Devine.

Penny cheered up as she read the words. She had always wanted to have a torch, one which she could take with her wherever she flew. The batteries in this light were everlasting.

As if the scene set was not bad enough already, Devine revealed the dreaded picture of Bully Bear. With this, even Oscar got his feathers ruffled as that cowardly bully always looks bigger than he really is. Oscar had flashbacks to his young school days. If it wasn't for the fact that Oscar was different from the other birds because he loved the truth, it would have been his wire-rimmed glasses perched on the end of his nose that made him the peck of all jokes.

In a cold sweat they all moved in closer to Devine. Devine turned the focus away from Bully Bear's sharp teeth and long claws and aimed it on something far bigger and greater than a bully's growl. "God's Word is your shield, so if you do feel afraid, hide behind it. This is your protection."

Proverbs chapter 30 verse 5

"No bully can get past what these words say," responded Devine most definitely. "Now, hold on tight to your shield, the manual, because you need to meet LuSINda, the tooth-less lion," said Devine.

Penny shrilled at the top of her tiny lungs, "LION, no one said there were going to be LIONS!"

"Don't worry," said Devine in a firm but calming voice as another feather fluttered to the ground.

Philippians chapter 4 verse 6

Devine reassured Penny, "I think you need to feel this feather, Penny, and use it as a bookmark in the manual." Clutching onto the words and the feather, Penny let Devine continue. "Now, I said *toothless* lion. She may look scary but she can't bite." Devine went on, "LuSINda has had her teeth taken out and can only make loud noises. Jesus went into the mouth of the grave but the teeth of death could not hold him. Jesus took out the power, the teeth, by rising again to eternal life.

Never forget, you can't keep a good bird down. So there's nothing to fear with this pussy cat LuSINda."

"Cat!" shrieked Melody. "My second worst fear is that purring pussy cat. They eat little birds like me for breakfast!" This reminded her of the ginger cat that used to stalk her street at home.

Devine stroked Melody with the feather of words given especially for this situation. As he did, all of those anxious thoughts just melted away like the snow which was beginning to disappear from the ground. The Glides were fully attentive to understanding the dangers they would face along the way, but they dropped their beaks in horror at the next photo.

"Take special care with the Night Wolf," said Devine. As they stared at the dark image in the picture, they all struggled to make out the outline of the Night Wolf, so Devine gave them a little more guidance:

Matthew chapter 7 verses 15 & 16

In the manual the Night Wolf really came to life and, in many ways, was the most dangerous of all. The Night Wolf knew every trick in the book as he had been trained well by his master Vermont.

Devine explained, "His eyes illuminate in the darkness with a vibrant yellow electrifying beam. He carefully lies hidden away, waiting for his time. He comes in different disguises. Sometimes he mixes up what he says with a bit of truth, just to try and take you off the scent of his trickery. So, this is very, very important: check out every word you hear against the words in your manual, and watch where the compass points to."

The morning sun was in full blaze and had melted the snow into a gentle river of water under their claws. They stopped for a cool refreshing drink to wet their dry tongues. The thought of the enemies they might meet on their journey had dried their mouths but they were not put off by the slideshow of fearmongers.

There was still one more enemy to be faced. Devine pulled out what looked like the sulky snake's cousin, but this prowler had short hairy legs. He was green and looked slimy, just like his nature. He had devilish eyes, a poker-red curling tongue and a strange lumpy mole on his chin, out of which grew one random, wiry hair.

"Meet Wiz the lying lizard, a spellbinding wizard. He wafts his tongue like a magician's wand, so you must stay free from his lies. You must not fear what his tongue may speak; there is nothing he can do to you. His words cannot cast a spell over you. They have no power if you choose not to listen. You must fear Father God and no one else. Not because he will ever try to make you afraid, but out of respect for him. Do what the Father says and you will be safe, with nothing or no one to fear."

With that, Devine put the snapshots away in the back of his manual as a reminder of where the whole story will one day end.

Melody sang a melancholy song and on a sad note wondered if there was a lyric that would carry her home.

"Home?" cried Devine, knowing what Melody was thinking. "You must not look back. Anyone who does is not fit for the journey. Behind you is a storm-battered city that was once your home, but ahead is the blazing glory of the Father's homeland, an eternal city." Then, in a poetic manner, he read them a description of what the dazzling eternal city will look like:

Isaiah chapter 54 verses 11 to 15

"I'm about to rebuild you with stones of turquoise,
lay your foundations with sapphires,
construct your towers with rubies,
your gates with jewels,
and all your walls with precious stones.
All your children will have God for their teacher,
what a mentor for your children."

(from The Message bible)

Finding a dry patch of ground to sit down on with his students, Devine turned their attention to what lay ahead.

"Now, before we carry on to the green hill far away, come to the 💚 Hideaway I told you about, the secret place found in your heart where you spend time with the Father," said Devine. He smiled and explained, "As you sit quietly, you will need to find the 🌳 Eternal Fruit Garden and take the fruit of truth from the Tree of Life. This is so that you can carry the character of the Father within you, becoming more like him. He will hold you steady so that you will never believe or tell a lie. The evil genius Vermont is the father of lies. Father God is all truth. So come away to the garden and taste of his character. Spend time getting to know him. Pause and glide in the truth of who your Father is."

Excited by the opportunity, Penny quickly grabbed her 🧭 compass and it pointed to a pear tree marked "truth". They went over to it and Oscar reached up with his beak and picked a pear for each of them. Then they looked up the following words in their manuals:

 Hebrews chapter 4 verse 12

"A sword sharpened on two sides, hmmm, I see, something that cuts between right and wrong; things that do or don't last," Oscar pondered. Then he exclaimed, "That's what God's words do." He was quickly becoming a fine student.

Then the penny dropped into the little sparrow's heart as she declared, "Well I never, I want his truth sewn on my wing so that I will always follow and choose what is right."

"Amazing," sang Melody, "can we stay in the garden and nibble on this truth for a while?"

It was here in the garden that they soon forgot the images of those who would try to come against them. They were beginning to feel more confident on the inside.

Devine peeled open a ripe green pear and cut it into two halves, saying, "Come close to me and let's look at the story of Jesus in the Garden of Gethsemane, a special garden he visited just before he died on the cross." Devine whispered, "Here he prayed so hard that he sweat splashes of blood onto the ground. In this garden, Jesus had to make the hardest choice of his life: would he choose the way of this world – today's fame and fortune – or would he choose his path marked out to Blazing Glory, the eternal way where he would give his life for you? Jesus's path to Blazing Glory was to die so that he could take upon himself the punishment for all the sins of the world. What a hard choice. What the Father had asked him to do cut through his heart. That was the price

Jesus had to pay to build the road of truth on which others could follow him to Blazing Glory."

The three Glides dropped their beaks in sheer amazement as Devine continued, holding up the two segments of pear. "Jesus could pick up the fleshy half and take the easier way of the world, but if he did that he would not see Blazing Glory. Or he could choose to take the other half of the pear, the way of the spirit, which is guided by my wing. By doing this, he would make the way for you to be free of sin and to make Blazing Glory your homeland forever too."

Overcome with a flurry of excitement Oscar cried, "Wow, I'll take a bite of that truth!"

Sniffling in the corner of the garden was Penny. She whimpered, "Was there no other way than to die on the cross on the green hill? Surely there was no need for Jesus to suffer all that pain?"

Devine sighed and said, "No other way. No one else was good enough. All the wrong things done on the earth amounted to a huge price that no one else could pay. Only Blazing Glory could afford the cost and it had to be the Father's only Son, Jesus."

Staring into Devine's deep blue eyes Oscar reflected and said, "No wonder Jesus said his eye was on us. We cost him so much pain and suffering."

The next feather echoed Oscar's thoughts:

⸙ Romans chapter 3 verse 23

Coming away from the far corner in the garden, Penny sighed as she tripped over a twig. "How many times have I fallen and yet Jesus still died for me?" she said, picking herself up off the ground.

"Hmm," agreed Devine, "but if Jesus had not stooped down to you in your gutter, how could he have reached out his arm to save you?"

Melody bellowed, "Can we go to the green hill soon as I must go and sing my thanks to Jesus there?"

With a rush of happiness Devine quickly sewed truth badges onto each of their wings, and then they took off to the green hill.

With the friends having spent the best part of the day in the garden, evening began to dim the sky. One of the night prowlers came out early with his truth radar. He hid himself on the ground under a bush. It was the deadly Night Wolf. He launched arrows at the Glides which went hurling through the air as they flew off in formation. Each arrow fired at the Glides miraculously turned around and backfired

into the forming darkness. Night Wolf scurried off into the shadows, chased by his own weapons of war.

A day in the life of the Dupes had not been very productive at all. Delilah had led the party of Dupes in hot pursuit of Vermont. Shrouded by his cloak of darkness, he had promised that he would give her designer bags with any label she desired. Delilah was selfish and marched the troops down every bag trail until she found today's accessory. Driven by desire, they followed Vermont's lies, stumbling down a dark winding path. There was no light surrounding Vermont, and with no blaze of glory in the direction they were heading, who would light their way to safety?

The Dupes' claws were sore from walking on the ground and not flying in the air. Who should be lurking in the hidden places but Stavros, the sly fox with a saliva problem. Something caught Delilah's eye. She was impressed by his fur tail.

"That would make a splendid cosy foxy scarf," thought the fashion-conscious Miss. Without a thought for Charlie and Jack she marched them into the net of lies which would hold them all back from flying away. Well, at least until Vermont chose to let them go free. That is, if they ever could be free. With no warning of the fox's tricks from their deceiving leader Vermont, the Dupes had to listen to the drivel of Stavros for the whole evening. The foam from his mouth stuck to his whiskers. This gave a damp and dreary ending to the Dupes' first day of adventures.

The sunset began to paint a glorious picture as the Glides, still flying high, arrived at the green hill far away. With an aerial view Oscar noticed, as the moon cast its shadows, that some rocks on the hill seemed to create the image of a skull.

He began to shudder as he came to realize the full truth of what had taken place there. Penny and Melody were shaken by the vibrations of his wing, and were thankful that the flight would soon be over for that day. Penny was tired. She kept blinking her eyes, trying to stay awake like the bigger birds. She checked the arrow on the ⊕ compass. It had remained steadfast towards "truth" as they touched down. The three Glides landed safely on the carpet of green grass. They found and sank into a soft dry blanket of grass. Before they closed their eyes they opened their Bibles and read:

Romans chapter 6 verse 23

"Eternal life? What does that mean?" asked sleepy Penny, stretching and yawning.

"It means never ever ending, on and on and on again, forever," sang Melody rushing through exhilarating scales of delight.

Oscar pronounced, "We just need to kneel here and say a prayer before this day is over. Devine said that Jesus never goes to sleep, so he will be listening." Oscar earnestly led the others in 🕯 prayer:

"Father, please forgive us for the times we have not been true to you and what you say. We are sorry for all the wrong things we have done, and from today we want to be as free as a bird to live in your truth. We thank you, Jesus, that you paid the price for each one of our sins and we receive the forgiveness found here at the cross. We receive you – the truth – into our hearts and we know that through you we now have eternal life. We pray that your Holy Spirit will live in us and guide us in your way safely to heavenly Blazing Glory."

"Amen," agreed Melody and Penny.

They went to sleep, closing their eyes like curtains on the huge black starry sky. Hidden in their hearts were all the words that had become 💎 priceless treasure. This treasure was stored up to help them face whatever tomorrow might bring.

4
Humble Pie

The sun began to climb over the green hill, stretching its rays like long arms into the morning. Oscar opened his eyes, disturbed by the light and unsure of what he had nesting on his chest. He fumbled around for his glasses and saw that Melody and Penny had snuggled on the soft feathers covering his large belly. It was a first class mattress. "What a picture," he thought.

Whilst musing over the restful scene his attention turned. He was gripped by the vision of the cross which stood on top of the hill under the spotlight of the sun. The cross had cast its shadow over where they lay. Oscar gave a big sigh which caused his belly to expand and rise like a mountain. Melody and Penny woke and tumbled down onto Oscar's wing. In a stunned sleepy silence they all stared at this historic site.

Devine flew over where they were sitting and perched himself on a wooden beam of the cross. The Glides flew in closer to take a bird's-eye view, landing on the other beam of the cross. They peered down at the holes in the wood and the red stain of blood in the grain. Devine explained how extra long nails were used to pin Jesus to the cross. They were so long they were just like the arrows that had been fired at the Glides by the Night Wolf. The Glides noticed a quiver in Devine's voice as he described the piercing thrust that had most sharply hit the side of the target, Jesus.

"The arrow-like nails were driven through the wood, scarring the hands and feet of your greatest friend forever. A random arrow even hit him from the side and broke through his heart. Blood and water poured out to stain this hill of sacrifice," explained Devine with a strange anticipation in his tone.

Penny, confused and with her heart pounding, asked, "Why was he lifted up and made so ugly before all his Creation?"

Devine directed them to the pages in the Bible so they could see the love of the Father on full display:

John chapter 12 verse 32

Devine then answered, "Because it's for everyone to see, so that all can be drawn in by his love."

Melody took off all in a spin and felt quite giddy from all the messy detail. She hit the ground and then began to roll down the green hill. She took a tumble right to the bottom, where long grass grew.

Who should be lurking in the long grass but Cyril the snake. He had come to rattle her bird cage so that she could not fly free. With deceiving words he spat out poison from his slimy tongue. "How can something so messy be good?" commented Cyril, unable to look at the cross himself. "Jesus didn't look that strong and powerful, did he?" With a long hiss and a cunning smile he said, "Are you sure it was meant to be that way, because if the Father is so good, why did he let bad things happen to his Son?"

With the poison of his words Melody began to wail. The grass swayed where she was but Melody could not be seen from the top of the hill by the others. Devine could sense her danger and called out with a plan to lift her out of the long grass crying, "Sing, Melody, sing! Cyril's words will only keep you down. Raise your voice to God and your spirit will rise and fly you up to safety."

Melody began to sing and worship God and was lifted up so she could see her way back up the green hill. Cyril slithered away through the long grass, hissing, to wait for another opportunity.

Devine caught Melody with a wing hug and called the Glides together. "After that brush with danger I think it's time to go to the Hideaway. The angry fowler, that evil genius,

waits around in the morning to try and trick and treat you off
the path to Blazing Glory, so you must learn to start the day in
the 💚 Hideaway," said Devine putting his claw down firmly.

Wanting to make the most of every spare minute Oscar
replied impatiently, "But the day has already begun and
there's so much to discover."

"You won't get your claws off the ground unless 🪔 prayer
lifts you up. Come, pause and glide here. Listen to what
Father has planned for your journey today," smiled Devine.
Devine raised his wing and they all settled down to be still
and quiet.

Miles off course, the three Dupes were still caught in the
net of lies. They were raging; raging with hunger and double
raging because they had been trapped into doing what they
did not really want to do.

"How will we ever get out?" sobbed Delilah, "I need a bird
bath. Look! All my feathers are in such a mess."

"We wouldn't be in this mess if we had bought our flight
bags from camp. We don't have our manuals or our compasses. How will we ever find the way?" repeated Charlie over
and over again.

With a sudden wing flap, Vermont viciously swooped down,
"WAY, WAY, WAY, who said the forbidden word 'WAY'?"

"It must have been Jack," accused Charlie and with his beak
continuing to fire at him. "He's always saying the wrong thing
in the wrong place, forever digging around in someone else's
nest. Jack wanted the manuals and compasses for his collection of objects."

"I'll have no more mention of those objects!" shouted
Vermont in a billow of thunder. The feathers on the Dupes'
backs stood up on end in fright. They looked like they had

overdone their hair gel. Seeing that he may have overstepped
the mark with his fearmongering, Vermont turned down the
volume to lure them in with a gentler, softer approach. "Look,
forget the things you were told. I've found some good soft
soil. We can dig around for some juicy worms and then
we can have a scary-packed, I mean fun-packed, day as we
discover more treats," said sly Vermont.

"As long as I can have a bath first," pleaded Delilah.

Tied into another day of trouble, the Dupes followed
Vermont deeper into the darkness. Flying low to the ground
they dodged through the trees. The patterns and lines on the
bark of the tree trunks looked like fearsome faces and images
that would certainly keep them awake at night.

Meanwhile, sitting patiently listening in prayer, the Glides
had lost all track of time. It had just flown away, along with
all their thoughts of trouble. They were thinking about the
words found on this feather:

Philippians chapter 4 verses 7 & 8

Devine gently coughed, waiting for them to finish pecking
at their morning's words of life, then spoke: "Stay in the
increase of the Father's peace. It will keep you focused
on the way he wants you to go today. Now it's time to find
the Eternal Fruit Garden. If you are to take the path to
Blazing Glory then you will need to carry your cross."

Matthew chapter 10 verses 38 to 40

After studying the words in his manual through his bent
glasses Oscar interrupted, "Why do we have to say no to the

things we want in order to follow Jesus? Why can't I go my own way and save myself? I have a wing-span greater than anyone and I am really strong." Oscar flexed his toned wing muscles but Devine was not impressed.

Devine raised his voice and said, "Stand in line, Glides!"

Feeling his rebuke Oscar, Melody and Penny flew to his command at once.

Ephesians chapter 2 verse 8

Devine gave them what was to be their daily trill drill. "Each journey you make starts and finishes at the foot of the cross. Here you all stand equal and in need of the same amount of the Father's help, which is called grace, to make it to Blazing Glory. The only way you are even able to catch a glimpse of this spectacular light is through the window of the gospel, the good news in your manual. Through it you can look love in the face and have a reason to hope for the future."

Melody and Penny felt taller on the inside and swiftly hopped up onto Oscar's shoulder. They were all the same in the Father's eyes. Some small and others tall, with different-coloured feathers to set them apart, but all were equally important to Father God.

"Imagine this," said Devine. "Jesus had the highest place in Blazing Glory. He was of equal importance to Father God. Jesus humbled Himself, made Himself of no great reputation but left that dazzling kingdom and covered up his kingship with the disguise of an ordinary man. Jesus then became obedient to his Father's great plan for him to die on the cross."

Looking as puzzled as each other, they all shouted "Why?" at the same time.

"To show his love to his Creation, so that you could be his friend, one with the Father. That also means one with each other, all living for that common vision and purpose to lead others home to Blazing Glory. That will involve denying yourself, putting the needs of others first. Carrying your cross means doing whatever Father God has planned for you to do, whatever the cost. The cross will only have its power if you carry it in the same way that Jesus taught you to," instructed Devine.

Feeling tiny in size, each of the Glides knelt as they humbled themselves to the call made by Devine.

"Eating humble pie when you don't deserve a crumb is a very noble thing," chirped up Oscar.

After having their bright yellow banana badges sewn on, they were fit for purpose.

"Quite stunning in fact," thought Melody as she examined its delicate detail. "Why is the fruit of humility a banana?" munched Melody, as she threw the skin away over her shoulder.

Penny rushed forward showing off her new badge and "Arghhh!" She slipped and slid on the skin right to the bottom of the green hill.

Oscar chuckled, "Pride always comes before a fall. I think it's always best to humble ourselves before someone does it for us. Even on our proudest day we can look quite foolish."

Penny well exceeded the sparrow speed limit as she rolly-pollied down the green hill quicker than even the fastest Olympic sparrow. Her feathers were an unsightly dirty brown, plastered with sticky mud. How could she, from such a place of ecstasy, now find herself in a heap of dirt? From high up in an oak tree a jolly mockingbird thought he would add music to the tale, singing, "We will, we will mock you".

Hanging her beak low, Penny found a safe bush to hide in and draw her twittering breath, when suddenly a feather soothed her pain:

Matthew chapter 10 verses 29 to 31

Adding ointment to her wounds, Penny waited whilst Jesus's words healed her. Her fall was not caused by his hand, but he was caring for her. This was so that she would learn to wrap her wings around others in their sorrow. Comforted and loved, she wanted to hold onto this feather forever. She made it a prize bookmark, keeping it warm between the words in her Bible that her Father had spoken to her.

Watching from the top of the green hill, Melody had found the whole scene a bubble of fun and so popped and rocked the morning away in praise, forgetting the value of little Penny who had taken a tumble. Father had seen Penny's great but common spendable value that would become treasure in his kingdom.

Oscar turned away from the commotion; he was not into frivolity and nonsense. He thought he would ride a few currents of air to take a bird's-eye view of the green hill and spy out what lay ahead. "My, how big and brave I have become," he thought as he soared to new learning heights. "I'm in altitudes of brilliance," continued Oscar, as his head swelled with pride.

Devine kept watch on the situation, keeping his wing of covering in place but letting lessons be learned by experience. He always let his students fly free. "It is no use them carrying their cross if they are not going to hold it the right way," thought Devine. "They will have to learn this lesson the hard way."

Oscar rested on a white fluffy cloud and did some extra homework, reading through the manual:

 Luke chapter 10 verses 25 to 37

As he finished reading the tale, the cloud burst in a shower of light rain. Oscar dropped from a great height right to

where Penny lay. Whilst her feathers were in a sticky mess from her fall, her heart was in a state of feathered bliss. Looking at Penny's humble state Oscar learned the lesson of the kind of heart Father looked for in his children: a heart like Father's own. Oscar understood how he, even though on a noble pursuit of learning about God, had forgotten to behave like God. Which was most important to Father? Which would be of greatest value when he finally reached Blazing Glory?

A great treasure was found by Oscar that day. From his high seat of learning he stopped and stooped like Jesus would expect him to, to find the hurting and broken. He carried Penny lovingly on his back to the green hill where she would be made completely well and clean. He placed her down next to Melody who became a little jealous because she had only won one jewel so far. She could not understand why Oscar and Penny had more. Melody thought she would gain them through her gift of singing. She had perfected her singing talent but now needed to perfect her heart. The gift given is not the prize itself. The value is in the way it is used to win an eternal reward. Melody would one day learn this lesson so that her song could be remembered in Blazing Glory. Oscar wrapped his wings around his two little friends and they scurried through the grass to where Devine stood.

"Well now," said Devine excitedly. "Are you ready to take up your cross on the flight plan of justice?" He paused as he glanced at each of them in turn. "Our mission is to carry hope into every corner of the world: to the poor and injured, bringing God's justice to their needs as we go," explained Devine. "Only humble hearts will be able to carry its true weight, so make sure you are travelling light. No selfish attitudes."

With their flight bags firmly on their backs, Oscar took off with Melody and Penny safely perched on his back. Devine bowed his head, looking once more at the cross, and followed the Glides on their important mission.

5

Flight for Justice

From deep within the dark and dingy woods, the three Dupes were startled by the roar from the Red Arrow formation high in the sky. Vermont nose-dived to the ground, quickly followed by Charlie, Jack and Delilah. They all ended up with their beaks stuck in the mud, and unfortunate Delilah could not pull hers out of the soil. Jack refused to help Delilah as his bag had burst open and scattered all his priceless bits of shiny paper onto the floor. The bits and bobs swirled around in the breeze, creating a paper shower. Jack had to catch each one with his frustrated beak. Charlie decided he would be a young gentleman and help Delilah. He wrapped his wings around her waist, paused for a moment as he quite liked her, then "pop!" Her beak became free and they both tumbled onto a pile of leaves. This annoyed Jack even more as his treasure of shiny paper blew even further into the woods.

The Glides flew over the spooky trees with Devine at their tail. They were the Red Arrow formation, pointing in the ⊕ direction of truth. Their wings were spread out for humility and justice. This was quite a triumphant sight indeed. They were charged with these words:

🔭 Psalm 45 verses 3 to 7

Red smoke painted the clear blue skies and the quest could not be hidden from the world below. The Glides were on course to Blazing Glory, led by a cloud and a pillar of fire.

Vermont stomped around in fury as he could not bear to look at the truth, especially painted in red. It reminded him too much of the day of his empire's defeat. That history-making day over two thousand years ago was gaining powerful momentum. It gave Vermont vivid flashbacks to rewind to those fatal hours in his mind. The doom in the tomb that was set to hold Jesus down had backfired with a blast. Jesus had risen right before their eyes with the unmistakable truth that death could not keep him a prisoner. Jesus was free to lead those who would follow him home to Blazing Glory.

The Dupes were becoming more and more troubled with Vermont's fowl moods. He never told them the real reason why he was an eternal loser.

"Why are your feathers in such a mess, Vermont?" questioned Delilah, brushing the leaves from her coat. "Would you like me to shampoo and condition them for you?" She was trying to calm his apparent torment.

Vermont was not amused and went off for a secret meeting with his six dastardly aides, the cruel stalkers. Not satisfied with just holding down the Dupes, he was not going to give up until he had shot down each of the Glides. In fact, Vermont vowed never to give up on stopping any flight to Blazing Glory. Not at least until the day he would be sentenced to retreat into the torment of his own forever darkness, and the scorching fire that awaited him and his followers.

The word on the ground was loud and clear to bring the three Glides down.

The word in the air was carried by  prayer. The Glides' flight mission rose high above any threat into the increasing  peace of Jesus.

"I think they should watch their beaks," pondered Devine, "because when Father God moves his big toe their plans will be squashed to the ground."

 Psalm 68 verses 1 to 6

Vermont ended his meeting with a surge of anger as he came out from the shadows of the trees' creeping branches. His six stalkers went off under his instruction to find a dark place and lie in wait, ready to pounce on the Glides. Vermont then wrapped his wings of darkness around his Dupes, who had just finished finding all Jack's treasure and had packed it securely into his bulging bag. The telltale tweet, Charlie, just could not help blaming the others. He had turned on the chick and accused Delilah of not bringing the flight bags with the Bibles and compasses in.

"Mine did not match my feathers and would do no good for my flight cred!" squealed Delilah in a rage.

Vermont, who was clouded with black fury and had red smoke coming from his vulture nostrils roared, "If I hear one more mention of that, that, that . . . book, you will be cooked forever! Shortcrust pastry pie! And as for the compass . . . I swear Blazing Glory is just a figment of a believer's imagination. It's just Playstation pie in the sky when you die. Shortcrust pastry pie! That's all any fowl pheasant is good for!"

Lowering his tone, Vermont proceeded, "Now my sweet, tweet little Dupes, take a treat from the bag. A couple of field mice, perhaps, or three and follow me to Bully Bear, I mean Brown Bear Country. I seem to remember it's quite near Orange County. Well, some kind of fruit place."

With a swirl of dust Vermont rose with his dominant wings. The Dupes had barely had a chance to tuck into their mouse brunch when they had to fly. Charlie was unable to finish chewing his delicate feast and accidentally choked on his final beakful. He coughed and spluttered as he took off, spitting out the morsel of mouse to the ground. Vermont was impatient and would not wait for anyone, so neither would his followers. Flapping as hard as their feathers could fly, they flew only centimetres off the ground.

It was quite the opposite for the Glides, who just never seemed to be in a flap. They soared on the wind as they were carried to their next destination. Devine noticed that the noonday sun was scorching young Melody's beak and decided that the flight for justice should land for fuel and refreshment. He caught a flight current below Oscar and directed the crew to a clearing in a pine forest. Oscar, with one eye on Devine and the other looking keenly at the ground, saw that it was not the most affluent of places. In fact, it was a bit shabby and poor.

"Seat belts on for landing," commanded Devine. Their flight formation touched down in this forgotten place. It looked neglected and bare, but had gained the attention of Devine. They found a patch where some colourful bluebells grew and settled down for a light lunch of a worm or two. Surrounded by the sweet aroma of the bluebell scent the Glides got out their trusted manuals.

Isaiah chapter 9 verse 2

They scurried through the pages of the Bible, and as the pages were fully opened a great light beamed out from between the words. It was a single glimpse, a moment's glance of the Blazing Glory that would one day become their home. The Glides gasped in wonder, not sure why they had been chosen to take part in this incredible journey. Suddenly, those living in the bare hollows of the trees came flooding into the light. There were all different varieties of creature. Some crept and others crawled but they had one thing in common: they were living each day with no reason to hope. A squirrel came out from the foot of a pine tree, scratching around trying to find out why his home had suddenly been filled with a warm glow. It seemed like the whole forest had gathered to see this remarkable sight. Shimmering through one of the blazing light rays floated a pure white feather:

John chapter 3 verse 16

Melody, moved by these simple famous words, sang a song all about Jesus, who was Father God's love come down, like a gentle feather, to reach us. Penny looked twenty centimetres taller as she stood to speak. She began to spend her worth as a broken vessel on those who listened. The Father had put her back together, piece by piece, and she had become a fine example of his gentle craftsmanship. With her heart mended from all the sadness that had broken her young life, Penny talked about her short but eventful adventures.

"From my many falls into the gutter of no hope, and lots of broken nests, Jesus has given me this brand-new life," said Penny as tiny teardrops splashed from the end of her beak. With gentle confidence she read out loud this verse from her manual:

2 Corinthians chapter 5 verse 17

"A new creation!" cried out a robin who was listening on a nearby branch. This robin normally said nothing as his breast had grown a funny yellow colour instead of the usual red, leaving him shy and withdrawn because he did not fit in. "I want to be brand new," said the robin as he flew down, unashamedly squashing a mass of bluebells with his rushed entrance.

So many came to the light that day and gathered like a feathered and furry flock around Devine. Devine gave them each their Bible and compass along with the instructions to go on their own personal journey with their new forever friend. He raised his wing and touched each one with this feather:

🪶 Acts chapter 1 verse 8

Stirred but not ruffled, the forest creatures all returned to their hollows which were no longer in darkness but filled with an extraordinary blaze of light.

Oscar sighed and said, "That was a real mercy flight, my friends." He was now walking around with a glow of delight.

Devine swooped in and said, "Yes but don't run down the runway and take off without having the mark of this mission firmly sewn on your wings. Come to the 🤍 Hideaway and taste the fruit in the 🐿 Eternal Fruit Garden. It's time for each of you to understand the Father's true heart for this quest. You may even discover a special jewel to invest in Blazing Glory."

Melody piped up, "I sang so well, I sang my feathers out, so do you think I will get one this time?"

Devine smiled at her courage but instructed them to wait.

Listening intently to him and 🕊 praying as they watched, they saw in front of their eyes the most luscious apple tree.

"God is a good God. No rotten maggots in him. He is perfect and made the world without imperfections," said Devine firmly.

"How did his Creation become spoilt and why do things and creatures grow old and die?" wondered Oscar.

Opening the manual right at the beginning, the Glides began to see what had happened to this beautiful world:

🔭 Genesis chapter 3

"That stolen bite of the apple at the beginning of time is where the Fall took place. This is where the way was lost to Blazing Glory. Humankind tumbled from perfection and spoilt Creation forever." There was a stunned silence. Devine continued, "It was because of humanity's wrong choice. Humans chose to believe a lie rather than the Father's truth and ate from the tree of good and evil. Before this, humans knew only good. But afterwards they knew evil, not just in their heads but it infected them and all Creation. That's what the fight was all about on the green hill." Devine became excited as he explained, "God's only Son Jesus was totally good. In him was no badness at all. He came to take the evil maggot of sin from your life and in order to do that he was nailed to a wooden tree sawn into a cross. Jesus took sin right back to the tree where the Fall took place." Devine paused and raised his wings towards the heavens and said, "Now you can take the 'good' from God himself and change to be 'good' like him."

Melody frowned. Knowing the Glides did not fully understand, Devine went on, "Jesus's death was not fair because he had never done anything wrong. But Jesus wanted to hand out justice to all those who would take his help, to all those who wanted to be free from sin. This was the only way as there was no one else good enough to die for your sin."

A tear formed in the corner of Penny's eye. There was more to know. The Glides listened intently as Devine spoke.

"Jesus came to help those who could not help themselves. He came to help sinners who were caught by the fowler's snare, locked up by Jail Bird; those waiting for their death sentence of caged darkness." said Devine. "Jesus, by taking the punishment for everyone else's wrongdoings, took the keys of death and unlocked the cage to let all who believe in him fly free to their new homeland in Blazing Glory."

Oscar gratefully took his fruit portion. As the apple of justice was sewn onto his wing, he became puzzled by why so many were caged up when they could so easily be free. He was determined to take the good apple of justice wherever he went so that all whom he met could taste how good God is and fly free because of Jesus. Taking off in delight, he could not help but do a loop de la hoop in his circle of endless freedom.

John chapter 8 verse 36

Melody came skipping over for her apple badge of justice but tripped over something quite sharp. "What was that?" she cried with harmonic alarm scales of pain. "Ouch, ouch, get it out! It's a thorn, ouch!"

Penny got her little beak and used it like a pair of tweezers, pulling out the thorn. They could not believe what Melody had stumbled on in the Eternal Fruit Garden.

"How can a circle of thorns be found in such a beautiful place? Pain and beauty just don't go together," said Penny.

Devine replied, "There is no beauty, no glory, without pain. How can you deliver justice if you have not been touched by the pain that others feel? They become just meaningless words if you apply the medicine without understanding and love."

"I want to be good but I'm just a small sparrow. Who would take notice of me anyhow?" sobbed Penny.

"Take notice," rebuked Devine. He picked up the crown of thorns and held it above his head and with a stern tone continued, "Take notice. See how God humbled himself when he stooped down to notice the injustice in his Creation. As he stooped, this crown was left by his only Son who gave up the wealth of Blazing Glory along with the rich crown upon his head. He then swapped it for this crown of pain and suffering. Jesus knew he would be trodden down by the injustice of this world's evil genius, the angry fowler who is also known as Satan."

The Glides shuddered with terror as they thought of their three friends who had been tricked by him and were now lost in his darkness.

Devine drew their attention back towards the light and continued, "The crown of thorns can be found in this garden so that those who come can share in Jesus's sufferings. But these sufferings are nothing compared to the glory in Blazing Glory."

Melody smiled. "Do you mean we will get a real crown when we get to Blazing Glory? How amazing!" Her face glowed more vibrantly than ever before.

"But what about the suffering, what does it mean?" asked Penny, looking towards the ground.

With a tear in his eye Devine replied, "To heal someone else's pain you must feel their pain. There is nothing more lovely than common feathers that soothe the grief that others suffer."

"Yes," responded Penny. "That means I can help others up, can't I?"

"Fly for justice, Penny, fly!" cheered Devine.

Isaiah chapter 58 verses 6 to 8

As keen as ever, Oscar pulled out his compass to check out which way they were to fly next. Devine concluded, "It's time to rest. Come here and make a nest around this crown and sleep. The Father always gives the ones he loves plenty of rest."

Melody snoozed away, still dreaming of the jewels she wanted to win. Penny quietly tucked her gem under her pillow, warm yet humbled that she was able to add another jewel to her growing collection in her eternal home. Oscar dusted his compass and put it away until tomorrow, pressing in as near as he could to Devine.

6
Love Match

Bully Bear was impatiently waiting in the woods for his victims to arrive. He found a nice picnic area in Brown Bear Country and set out a lush spread of gourmet bird seed, plotting to tempt the three Glides onto the bird table. Here he would pounce and bully them to the ground.

Vermont led his Dupes under a heavy dark cloud nearby. He was the mastermind behind Bully Bear's plan. He liked to keep a close evil eye on things as he did not trust anyone. Trust was not a word he understood or practised.

Delilah gave a long sigh. She could feel the darkness and it was making her feathers damp and limp.

Charlie chirped up a bit when he caught wind of today's teddy bears' picnic in the woods. "Yummy, lots of crumbs and leftovers. I can just keep flying back for more, as I love doing and saying things over and over again. I told you it would be good fun trailing the bag of treats. Who needs to see that glory city, Blazing whatever?" exclaimed Charlie.

Jack started to chirpy cheep up to hope for a better day. "Just think," he said, "everyone will be outdoors, away from their nests. That leaves them empty for me to pay a visit and fill my bag with treats. My shiny paper is looking a bit dull now and I need some new things for when I finally settle in my penthouse nest someday."

Vermont swirled around in a thunderclap, causing a few onlooking budgies to fall off their perches.

"That'll teach them to be nosey," accused cheeky Charlie as sharp as ever as he laughed at their fall. He didn't like budgies much; they reminded him of his small annoying cousins.

Vermont bellowed, "Dupes, you must remain hidden so that you don't give the game away. Just remember, the table prepared in the picnic area is not for you."

They all scurried off and decided to make a small camp-fire because of the chill in the air. There was always a chill in the air around Vermont!

"I can't seem to shake off this present darkness," Delilah shivered. "Are you sure tricks and treats were meant to be this way?" Delilah asked with a dither in her words.

"Well, the wrapping paper is shiny enough, so it must be good," Jack responded, trying hard to reassure himself.

Just away from the clearing of the picnic area Charlie collected dry twigs to make a camp-fire. Rubbing two sticks together violently, the Dupes tried hard to be good scouts, watching for the smallest spark of light to ignite the fire. Suddenly, as if by magic, there was a flicker of fire. So they decided to get warm and toast a few worms until the picnic had roared into action.

"I'm keeping out of the way of any Bully Bear, trust me. Stay unnoticed and you will be fine," said Charlie from experience. Charlie had often been bullied due to his coat of many colours. He had learned how to avoid being picked on, the painful way.

Waking to a very different setting, the Glides wondered what the new day would bring. Stretching her melodious feathers Melody welcomed in the morning with a repeating chorus of praise to her Creator God. Penny decided she would throw in her offering of thanks too, for what a penny can bring.

Well that fooled you! A true diamond of a song! Any sacrifice of praise to God is always well received in Blazing Glory.

Oscar, after cleaning his stately feathers, carried the Glides to meet with Devine who was already in a quiet deserted place. He was absorbing the creative reflections of a brand new day:

Lamentations chapter 3 verses 22 & 23

"Draw closer, my dearest friends," cooed Devine, echoing the words from this feather.

As they huddled in tight Oscar was asked to read their portion of life words for the day. Expecting a handful of seeds for breakfast, Melody's beak dropped when he got out the Bible.

Wise Devine noticed everything, "That comes after we first feed our character. The seeds and nuts are being roasted as I speak," he reassured the hungry birds who were going to have to wait a short while for their breakfast.

Psalm 23

Oscar began reading: "The Lord is my shepherd. . ."

Devine interrupted and said, "That's Jesus, he is the Good Shepherd."

When Oscar had finished reading the whole chapter aloud they all prayed. Next they received a trilling breakfast and headed off for the green pastures described in the psalm. Full and free the Glides took off into the bright clear sky.

"I spy with my little eye," played Penny, who often got a little bored travelling long distances. "How long until we get there?" asked Penny. She began to irritate Oscar just a smidge.

Devine called out from behind, "Look! The Good Shepherd with his sheepdogs Goodness and Mercy."

"Where?" responded Melody who began to twist and shout with excitement.

Oscar, as sharp as ever, noticed the still waters down below. "That is perfect for a cool refreshing drink," said Oscar. So they decided to make a stop off. Oscar made a swift and smooth landing.

Penny was the first to dive into the still waters for a long-awaited bird bath, and it wasn't long before the others followed.

"This is heavenly bliss," sang Melody, splashing around. "Can things get better than this?"

Devine was moved to use the opportunity to show them something more about Jesus. The Glides had decided to take up their cross at the green hill and follow Jesus, and there was something very important they needed to reflect on by the still waters.

Matthew chapter 3 verses 13 to 17

"To be a true follower you need to be baptized in water. It's a bit like taking a bath." said Devine. Penny's eyes widened. "Jesus always led the way by example to show us the things that are important to his Father," reassured Devine. "Blazing Glory awaits and this is all part of being prepared. When you follow Jesus in this way, you show to the world how you have had your sins washed from your life and have accepted the truth that Jesus died on the cross to take your punishment. Coming out of the water displays the fact that you too will be raised to life when you die, just like Jesus, ready for eternal life in Blazing Glory with Father."

John chapter 1 verse 12

They were each instantly transported to the Hideaway to be alone with Father and were brushed by the words he breathed over them.

"When can I be baptized like Jesus?" Oscar asked boldly.

"Am I old enough?" interrupted Melody.

"Don't forget me!" cried often-forgotten Penny.

"How can we ever forget you, little Penny?" they all replied.

They all stepped into the still waters and were immediately baptized by Devine whose feathers rested on them like a soft fluffy white towel. He was well pleased with his students.

"Ooooh, I feel like I could soar to the highest heaven," boasted Oscar.

"Not without us," said Penny and Melody together. They frantically hopped onto his back for the ride, not wanting to get left behind.

"Check out those straight paths down there," commented Oscar. "And use your 🧭 compass, Penny, to see if we are on the right flight path."

The compass twirled around and pointed to "the way".

"True enough," declared Penny.

"Weeeee," shrilled Melody. "This Blazing Glory trail is a blast!"

"Hang on a minute," said Oscar, as he soared ahead on full throttle. "What's that puff of smoke coming out of the trees?"

"Where?" asked Melody.

"Over there," pointed Oscar with his beak.

Careful Penny pointed out that this led them off the right path and was unsure whether they should investigate. Devine allowed them to make their own decisions, knowing that everything would work together for their good because they truly loved God.

Romans chapter 8 verse 28

They landed in the wooded area of Brown Bear Country. Penny quite timidly said, "It's a bit dark in here, I much prefer the light on the blazing path."

"Hey, what's this?" rapped Melody with a hip hop beat, as she read a notice on a large oak tree. "A teddy bears' picnic, and that can only mean one thing . . . lots and lots of crumbs!"

"Test it, test it!" yelled Penny, very alarmed. "Look, the compass is pointing out of here. I don't think that we should be here!"

Penny fumbled the compass back into her flight bag. As she did her confidence dropped. The others took off in a hurry and she was unable to keep up as she was in such a flap. Penny yelled, "Oh no, oh birdie, I'm lost!"

All alone, in what seemed to her like a dark valley with no one to help her, she became paralyzed with fear.

"This can't be right, this can't be of Father. Jesus said that in his love there would be no fear. Where's his love? I'm lost, what shall I do?" Penny flapped and flew but could not find the others. "Think Penny, think," she said to herself, trying to comfort her own fears, when from out of the clearing wafted in a dazzling white feather:

✒ 2 Timothy chapter 1 verse 7

"Power, love and he will make me unafraid. Come on, Penny, exercise your faith. These words live so that they can help you." She found a nearby branch to rest on and went over this morning's Bible reading from Psalm 23. Penny remembered the next bit of the instruction in the chapter: "You prepare a table before me in front of my enemies." What could that mean, she wondered.

No sooner had this thought flown into her heart than it got chased straight back out again by a big, big, yes even bigger, Bully Bear. Penny saw him coming and zoomed off into the darkness. The bully gave chase through the haunting trees. Penny flew as fast as her little wings could carry her. In the clearing she saw something. "A table, yes a table in front of my enemies," she quoted with rising confidence.

Landing safely on the platform she paused to get her breath back then anxiously nibbled some seed to gain strength. In her time of feeling so weak and vulnerable she found God's Word to be true. With a tear rolling down her beak she cried out, "What am I to do? If I had a dad, he would deal with the bully and carry me away safely. But I'm all alone in this world and I don't know if I will be able to escape."

Through the leaves she could hear Bully Bear approaching. The crunching leaves under his paws got louder and louder. Penny began to do the only thing that could lift her high enough out of his reach – she prayed. "Help!" It didn't seem quite long enough. Would it be enough to bring the protection she needed? She remembered the model prayer given by Jesus which her grandmother had taught her:

Matthew chapter 6 verses 9 to 13

"That's it!" she squealed with delight. "Our Father means 'our Father'; my forever dad. I've got a dad and he can rescue me from the bully."

As Penny prayed, a strong tower seemed to just appear in the distance, lit up by a glowing light. It was tall like a skyscraper with one small window and a door which was slightly ajar. She did an emergency take off and flew to it for safety. Penny flew through the opening in the door and as she did the door shut firmly behind her with a loud crash. She screeched to a halt, and was met by a most unexpected sight. Who should she find there but the other Glides. Quietly they all listened and they could hear two dogs barking in the distance.

"Ah, there you go. It's Goodness and Mercy," smiled Devine. "They never fail to show up, just in time. They're expert bear-fighters, you know. They can't resist a big Bully Bear for their sport."

Exploring their strong tower they found in its grounds the Eternal Fruit Garden, and ventured inside the gateway. The garden was full of luscious grapevines. On each vine were huge bunches of grapes. The grapes represented the everlasting nature of God's love.

"Oh no, these grapes have been crushed and they've stained the ground," declared Oscar, tip-toeing through the soggy mess.

"Yes," said Devine, "you would never have seen the Father's love if Jesus had not been crushed and bruised for your sin. It would never have been discovered. You would never have been rescued. His love had to be poured out like a drink," continued Devine.

Romans chapter 5 verse 8

"It's in the darkest valley, when you are most frightened and bruised that love can be seen. Think about it. How would Penny have realized who Father God was if he was not able to save her in her broken, lost state?" explained Devine. There was a silent pause as the Glides tried to understand. "Jesus paid the price for your sin with his own royal blood so that you can be part of his family. He was crushed like a grape and his life poured out for sinners."

They each received their fruit badge of love, knowing that this grape juice was a hard drink to swallow. Drinking the symbol of God's love, they all remembered what it cost Jesus and promised they would remain forever thankful and mindful of his love.

"How can we pour out his love to others?" enquired Melody. "Hmm, wait a moment. I feel inspired by a very ancient song:

"Love lifted me, love lifted me,
When no one but Christ could help,
Love lifted me, hallelujah.
Love lifted me, love lifted me,
When no one but Christ could help,
LOVE lifted me."

With that they were carried off on the wings of prayer to find someone to touch with God's love.

You may well be wondering about the Dupes' camp-fire. Whatever happened to that? Don't worry, with all that fear, doubt, darkness and damp around, the flame soon died out.

"In the darkness again?" smirked Vermont as he teased the Dupes. "Well you had better stay holding onto me. You all look too afraid to go anywhere," he taunted the young Dupes.

And so the night closed in, ending another day.

7

Currents of Joy

"I'm so excited," declared Melody as she woke. "I'm sure when we went to sleep last night we were promised currants and raisins for breakfast. Was I dreaming?"

"Devine has been up and about," Penny replied. "Even before the sun got up, I might add, so you never know what could be in store."

"There are no stores or shops around here silly," chattered Oscar.

Unfortunately, still in the dark woods with no fire to keep them warm, the Dupes were getting quite a different breakfast.

Matthew chapter 7 verses 17 to 19

"Rotten fruit!" yelled Charlie in disgust. "What have we done to deserve this?"

"It's what you haven't done," smirked sly Vermont, raising one dark eyebrow higher than the other. "Never mind, we'll mix it up a bit and make a nice fruit cocktail drink instead. That should cheer up your drooping feathers," said Vermont sheepishly.

"Something to take the edge off this dreary trail, I hope," said Delilah making her point. "All I know is, I need a shopping fix; and quick. This simple living is not up my street."

Trying to keep them off the scent Vermont distracted them, "Look, if we keep going there's a beach over that hill. You will be able to make a nest and catch a few warm sun rays. Maybe I will let you hang out for a short break."

Jack picked up his bag of treats in his beak and announced, "Great, lots of bottle tops to shine the sun on and some colourful shells for my treasured collection!"

"And I can get a sun tan!" joined in Delilah in the excitement of the moment.

"A tan, a tan," repeated Charlie, "Never mind a tan, we need a long-term plan. We need some kind of purpose to this trip."

Vermont suggested just the ticket, and sold them what was to be their next short-haul flight, "Life's a beach, lots of rest and play. No need to build for tomorrow, live for today." Then under his breath he sneered, "For tomorrow you die."

Sold out good and proper they headed for the coast, wondering if their wings would carry them the distance.

"Well at least it's not a dark valley," thought Charlie to himself. In fact he thought about it over and over again, as really he was not one hundred percent convinced about Vermont. "There's just something about him I can't put my wing tip on," he concluded.

Meanwhile, the Glides tucked into the prepared breakfast carried in by Devine.

"Hey, look I wasn't dreaming. We have currants and raisins, yum yum. What a lovely feast to start the day," smiled Melody.

"Where did these come from?" asked Penny, who had never been offered such a posh treat before. A feather answered her curious questions:

Philippians chapter 4 verse 19

"Well, just how rich is our Father God?" enquired Oscar.

"Now, if the earth is the Lord's and everything in it and all things were made for his glory, what do you think Oscar?" answered Devine.

"Blazing rich!" squawked Melody.

Devine, noticing the sun rising even higher in the sky, needed to hurry the birds up as they had quite a flight ahead of them.

"Eat up, Glides, as you will find out today that the real current of joy isn't found in what you think. Father's joy is unspeakable. In fact, you haven't even heard the half yet," said Devine.

If all of the truth had been told that day they would have been there for an eternity so they sang and then prayed the hour away. Then, hopping onto a warm air current they took off and were carried off to distant shores.

The white fluffy clouds seemed to peel back like a long corridor to let the Glides through. As they hit the clear blue skies, Oscar looked down at a golden sandy beach. Hoping this would be the landing spot, he asked Penny to check out the way from the compass. It turned around in a hot spin and pointed to "life".

"Life is found up there on the rock," Devine said.

Steering the Glides on course, Oscar gave a loud instruction to his wing passengers: "Prepare yourselves, it may be a hard landing."

As soon as they touched down, Melody put on her Performer designer glasses and peered over the side of the high rock. "Cooee," she called to the Dupes below, who had taken a short cut and arrived at the beach ahead of the Glides. The Dupes couldn't hear as they were far away and busy making a holiday nest. Melody swiftly told the others she had found the long-lost Dupes.

Devine warned them all sternly to stay on the rock as the tide and currents of this world were not safe for them.

Down on the golden sands the Dupes were having a blast. Perched on his stripy red sun lounger and sipping water on ice – shaken but not stirred – Vermont was drawing up a cunning plan. He cooked up his next bag of tricks under his parasol and then lay back, allowing his mind to think on more devious plots of trouble. Delilah made her dream sandcastle whilst Charlie busily copied everything she did. He quickly became the annoying next-door-neighbour.

Jack was having none of that kind of nonsense and so tirelessly made a nest of comfort to settle down his ruffled feathers for the day. Stupidly, as he lay roasting himself in the sun, the heat intensified and he fell asleep, snoring loudly. The rays hit his shiny bits of bottle tops and the pieces of glittering paper woven into his nest. It wasn't long before his yellow beak turned a bright poker red. He woke in a flame of pain and fury. Jack jumped up and rushed towards the sea with his wings flapping, to cool his beak down in the breaking waves on the sea shore. It looked like a sauna as steam clouded all around his face as he dipped his beak into the clear blue waters. Charlie had an idea to help him.

"Turn your nest over and use this twig to hold it up. It will make a safe shade. I think you'd best shade here for the rest of the day," chuckled Charlie at Jack's burned face.

Vermont rolled over as he could not bear to go near anything hot, especially as hot coals were something he was trying to avoid. God had told him that his destiny was a lake of hot burning fire.

The Glides felt safe and cool on their solid rock. A cool breeze blew away any heat trapped in their feathers. Overhanging branches above the rock provided shade from the strong sun.

🔭 Psalm 62 verse 2

As they stood on the truth of God's words they felt their hearts become brave and strong. With confidence, not in her physical worth, Penny bowed her head and raised her wings in praise to her Father. Melody began to bang out a new rock beat with her beak, whilst Oscar stared knowingly out to sea.

Oscar was captured by the rays of the sun as they shimmered on the water. "Ah Blazing Glory, I can't wait to cross over there," he thought in a moment of reflection.

Devine gave a cooing call to assemble the Glides together and said, "There is going to be a storm, so it's time to hide yourselves away until the storm has passed. There's a gap in the rock over there where you can be safe."

Following his lead, they each huddled into the slight gap in the strong grey rock. It was a great adventure for them as the gap led into a cavern where they made a den. There was enough light seeping through the hole so that they were not afraid. It wasn't long before the winds picked up and hit gale force, and thick dark clouds drew across the sky like a curtain to block out most of the daylight. The rain pounded heavy and hard on the rock. The Glides were feeling a little uneasy. Their hearts began to flutter with the advancing storm. Devine stroked their brows with his wing of peace and spoke words of comfort so that the storm outside would not disturb their hearts.

"Now is the time to hide yourself deeper in the 🌳 Eternal Fruit Garden where you will discover God's ever-increasing 🌀 peace," said Devine.

Immediately, in the secret place, they closed their eyes and their minds to the things around them. The storm outside still raged like a torrent but could not come into this special place. They waited for Father's peace to fill their hearts and stood calmly in the eye of the storm. Here they found that incredible stillness of God's abiding presence.

"This is where God is found. He will be found by anyone who looks for him, no matter where they are or what trouble they find themselves in," whispered Devine.

🔭 Deuteronomy chapter 4 verse 29

They opened their eyes and a large red strawberry began to grow right in the centre of their group. It was a burning red colour, with a soft bumpy skin. The little dimples in the strawberry gave it a cheeky happy smile. Devine gave them each a portion to eat whilst he told them one of Jesus's well-known stories from the Bible.

🔭 Matthew chapter 7 verses 24 to 29

"Jesus is the rock. He is the foundation your lives must be built on. Only his words are true and trustworthy." explained Devine. "You cannot avoid the storms that hit your life, but your hope will be steady as you stand firm on the rock, Christ

Jesus. If the situation around you makes you totter from the fear of trouble, look for the gap in the rock. The gap is the shelter of his words. His words will keep you unharmed and you will come out changed by what you see the Father do for you. You will grow bigger and stronger to fly another day."

They each received their strawberry smiley badge of joy which was carefully sewn onto their wing. The sweetness of the taste of the strawberry took away any thoughts of the storm that was now beginning to die down. They were dressed with the words that a feather carried to them:

Colossians chapter 3 verse 12

Each of the Glides was being hand dressed with their Creator's designer label. The strawberry badge brought such colour and fun to each of their wings.

"You are being changed by the Father's nature as he dresses you to live the way he designed and wants you to," explained Devine.

Penny looked at her glowing coat and spread out her wings. Her common brown feathers were slowly being transformed into something quite stunning. She loved her new image because it was just like Father's. They each cherished what had been given to them. They were determined to spread their wings with joy so that others could see their happy good deeds and so glorify the Father.

 ## Matthew chapter 5 verse 16

With the storm over and the clouds left as puddles on the ground, the Glides were ready and dressed to continue their quest. Oscar pulled out the compass to determine the way. It pointed to the "way", towards the estuary where the river flows into the sea. They had learned the lesson of how to rise above the storms of life with the incredible joy given by Jesus. Now they were ready to flow into the eternal river of peace waiting down the way. Devine let them see a glimpse of Blazing Glory as he described the river that came from the Father's throne.

"Only love and peace can flow towards his children, because Father's nature is perfect. Come and follow the river and pick the fruits which are everlasting," Devine said.

Hopping onto Oscar's back they were raised on this happy current of joy. It was totally different to what they expected it to be. Oscar smiled his biggest smile ever saying, "Well, the miracle of joy is that it is at its fullest when we are most empty and in need of it."

Melody laughed and said, "I want my heart to be like a large arena, with all that space for God to fill with his joy so that everyone can hear just how tip-top fantastic he is." She finally understood that the spotlight should be on her Father and not on her gift and so she won a priceless jewel.

 Philippians chapter 4 verse 4

From behind, Devine whispered a tale of reminder as this was to be a long flight but well worth the journey:

Acts chapter 1 & Acts chapter 2 verses 1 to 13

"Remember this reading next time you branch out and spread your wings for the gospel. You must carry the good news about Jesus wherever you go. When the events in these chapters took place, Jesus's followers were in the most danger they ever had faced without him being there in person," said Devine quietly. "He had returned to Blazing Glory and they felt empty and alone in the storm of hate against them. Father in Blazing Glory sent them his own storm of joy, me, Devine, to change the landscape forever. I am the tongue of fire spoken of in the reading. I am the Holy Spirit."

"I can't wait to land and study those chapters more closely," exclaimed Oscar, busy being the pilot of the flight.

Penny was tickled by a feather that floated down:

Psalm 16 verse 11

"Oh, fullness of joy when God is with you, skiperdy do dah," laughed little Penny.

As they flew on course over the rock towards the river they could see Vermont in the distance, clutching twigs from a nest in his beak.

"What's that?" exclaimed Penny.

"It looks like a jackdaw with a red beak. Hmmm, you don't normally get that variety of feathers around these parts, do you?" remarked Oscar.

"You do now," laughed Melody. "It's sun-fried Jack and the other two Dupes clinging onto Vermont for dear life."

"They won't find it there," sighed Devine sadly. "Come now, let's pray for them. Maybe they will find the path that leads to the way, the way to Blazing Glory."

8

Peace Like a River

The fountain of joy overflowing inside the Glides left a blazing trail in the wake of the storm. In the distance, peace like a river welcomed them forward. The ⊛ compass turned again and pointed to "life". Ahead they could see the river teeming with life and on the river banks were trees full of fruit. The trees had the most enormous green leaves. Devine said that the leaves, when touched, brought health.

"Is this Blazing Glory?" squealed Melody.

"Eyes have not seen, ears have not heard, nor has it ever been contained in a heart just how amazing it is there. This is just a sample peck, as it were, to keep you on course for Blazing Glory," said Devine.

"Can we land on its grassy banks and enjoy the peace of the river?" asked Oscar, a little tired from being the pilot.

"Hiccup, hiccup! . . . Oh dear," laughed Penny. "It's all that joy bubbling up inside, I can't stop . . . hiccup, hiccup." She was making the flight very bumpy.

"Hold your breath," instructed Oscar, who plunged into an emergency landing. Penny shuddered forward and back. "That'll do the trick," he smirked as the hiccups got left behind a cloud somewhere.

"Wonderful," burped Penny, which was the full stop on the hiccup.

The Glides found a lush green patch to rest for a while.

Clutched by the sharp claws of Vermont, the Dupes steered clear of the way. Charlie perked up, "Vermont, that's not the way."

"I'll do it MY way," jeered Vermont. "You must learn to trust me."

"But . . ." said Charlie.

"Silence!" shouted Vermont.

In silence they trembled, unable to voice what they knew to be true in their own hearts. Frozen by fear, they felt they had no option other than to go with the flow.

Delilah glanced behind towards where the Glides had landed and she welled up with tears. In the distance she had noticed the beauty of the badges sewn onto the wing feathers of her long-lost friends. The feathers seemed to be more beautiful than she remembered them. But it wasn't the feathers. It seemed to come from inside the Glides. With her head dropping, she splashed tears on her tatty and what was now becoming moth-eaten coat.

"What are you crying about?" yelled Charlie. He lacked any form of understanding.

"Nothing," sniffled Delilah. "It's just the cold wind in my eyes," she lied through her beak.

In the distance was another river. "There it is," called Vermont.

"The water is all muddy," exclaimed Delilah in disgust. "How will I ever get this coat looking anything like its former glory?"

With a loud thud Vermont dropped them to the ground. Jack looked up and all he could see was the world in a spin.

"Spinning around, I'm spinning around," sang Jack, spilling out that familiar tune he had heard on the radio.

"What on earth are those things up that tree?" asked Jack.

"Harps," discovered Charlie as he flew up onto the weeping willow.

"Harps? Since when did they grow on trees?" responded Jack.

"Since we arrived in Babylon," roared Vermont.

"BABYLON!" cried all three Dupes. "What are we doing in Babylon?" they asked, all in a state of shock.

"Stop fretting. Just for the record, it's in the beloved manuals you keep going on about. So there's nothing to worry about is there? Trust me."

Psalm 137 verses 1 to 4

True, it is in the manuals. The Bibles had been given to them so that they could always check the words for themselves. But without Devine to guide them and their manuals back at base camp, Vermont was able to trick them by not telling the complete truth. Babylon was not the way, nor the place, to find the "rest" of the Father. In fact, it was such a sad place. Those who loved God had been captured by their enemies and taken there many years before. They were the ones who had hung up their harps in the weeping willow trees, for they thought they had no reason to sing in this God-abandoned place. Along the muddy river bank they sat down with glum faces. Jack thought he'd help himself to a harp as no one was laying claim to them. He plucked out some clunky notes and annoyed the others with an out-of-tune jingle.

Delilah wagged her tail down by the banks of the muddy river. "This is bad beyond my worst expectations. No reflection, just thick swirling filth is all I can see. How on earth will I ever get my dignity and worth back? Why did we have to sell out for a bag of useless tricks and treats?" she wailed.

"Enough of that," demanded Vermont. "This route is much quicker." But where it was leading, he wasn't telling them.

"Good news at last. I can't wait to wake up from this nightmare. The quicker the better if you ask me!" shouted Delilah. "As long as I'm first in the bird bath I don't care."

"Don't care, don't care," repeated Charlie. Being a Dupe had certainly taken its effect on him.

Peace flowed like a river down the way, where the Glides were refreshed in the quietness of the moment.

Penny broke the silence with thought-provoking words, "Oh how I wish we could carry this river everywhere we go."

"Do you believe that is possible?" asked Devine.

Penny looked at her tummy and giggled. "My tiny tank's not big enough."

"What about your forever tank?" replied Devine.

"What do you mean by 'forever' tank?" replied Penny, looking for her belly button buried amongst her feathers.

John chapter 4 verses 3 to 14

This was the precise moment for Devine to draw the three Glides into the Hideaway, where the door was unlatched to the Eternal Fruit Garden. They were greeted by such a fine display of colour that they could not believe their eyes. The most enormous ripe peach was before them, ready to be eaten.

"Feel it," invited Devine. "Know how your Father has the most incredible power. There is no one greater than him, yet his peace is so gentle and soothing."

They tucked into this mouth-pecking, beak-watering lunch and listened, lost in the peace of the fruit they indulged in.

Devine went on to teach them more about Jesus. "See how, in this meeting, Jesus could have dealt harshly with the woman in the story. The woman was the lowest of the low. She was in a whole pile of trouble and was hiding her pain underneath the good-looking smile on her face." said Devine. "Jesus saw past the lip gloss and straight into her troubled heart which was desperate to find peace and be loved. He offered her an amazing drink found in the eternal river of life in Blazing Glory."

The tale brought tears to their eyes and as they dropped to the ground a feather drifted across the three Glides and wiped away their sadness:

Revelation chapter 7 verse 17

"What a place, where all tears are wiped away. I want to stand in the fountain of life as it flows right through the centre from the Father's throne. This must mean that the Father is the King too. Blazing bliss," responded Oscar. He was not too sure if it was okay for boys to cry.

Devine continued, "Look how the woman in the story took the drink deep into her heart. Inside her a well was opened up so that the living water could rise up to satisfy her thirst for life on the inside. She could have a drink whenever she needed it."

"What about when it runs out?" enquired young Oscar.

"Runs out?" smiled Devine. "It's an eternal spring, a forever supply, and I'm its source. And I get it from the fountain of life itself, Jesus. There was so much living water in the woman that she ran and told all her friends and they all came and received their own supply from Jesus for themselves."

Feeling thirsty, they all asked, "Can we have this river in our lives too?"

"Yes, just ask. You will need to sit still – that's quite important when you take a drink – and just ask Jesus." As they were still they were filled with living water and the well was declared "open all hours" by Devine as he sewed on their badges of peace.

Oscar was puzzled as to how it all fitted together. He liked to understand everything but some things are just beyond working out he soon realized.

Isaiah chapter 55 verses 8 & 9

"Trust and peace go hand in hand," he thought. "We trust God, holding onto his peace; this is a fabulous way to walk down the way!"

It took time for Devine to sew on Oscar's badge as he was full of so many questions.

Melody had flown off just outside the garden. Suddenly there was a loud screech. Long high notes rang into the undisturbed blue sky. They all dashed towards the noise and to their alarm it was Melody. Oscar thought she may have been doing some vocal training but it was worse . . . much, much worse.

"As if Melody's singing isn't bad enough already," thought Oscar.

"I've been bitten by a snake," Melody cried. "It was Cyril the sulky snake."

Cyril was bored with the tranquil state of the Glides and had decided to inject a bit of poison into his victim. The sly rattlesnake added his trickery to the truth, and bit Melody with lying words. Immediately, her leg began to balloon up and she performed a dramatic faint into the arms of Devine.

"What were you doing, Melody, listening to lies?" questioned Devine.

"He just seemed interesting. Snake-skin has always been a fatal attraction where girls are concerned," snapped Melody, not so melodious.

"Snakes always have the tricks to make victims fall," said Devine, a bit hot under the beak. "Quickly," he cried. "Use your wings of peace and come and comfort her, Penny."

"I think she needs a little more than comfort," responded Oscar.

"An antidote from a doctor, judging from the state she is in," said Penny, most concerned.

"No time to find a doctor," croaked Melody as Penny wrapped her wings of peace tightly around her.

The pain grew worse and Melody became deeply troubled. Devine knew he had no time to lose. He did not want Melody to go home to Blazing Glory before she had completed all the things that God had planned for her to do, so he instructed the Glides what to do next.

"The manual said you would be safe, even from bites from snakes," said Devine reassuringly as he hovered over the victim. "Melody, listen to me," Devine said firmly. "Remember the swirl of peace, close your eyes and get right into the centre of it. Father is right here, and that peace I have told you about knows no end." With assurance in his voice, Devine declared, "Father God is in control of this situation."

Devine then looked at Penny and said, "Penny, you pray for Father God to be her present help in her time of need."

He then turned to Oscar.

"Oscar, I want you to pray, calling on Jesus to heal her. His is the greatest name you can call on. He will be Melody's healer."

"What if my words are not heard?" said Oscar.

"Well don't use your words, use his. He hears all your prayers but, if you want to, you could also use the words found in the manual," replied Devine.

"But what if it doesn't work?" said Oscar, who was most certainly a student in training.

"It's for you to ask, believing in God, the one who spoke the words. He is the one who will perform the miracle. The pressure is off you. It's not up to you. Remember, trust and peace go hand in hand."

With a lump in his throat and stammering over his words, Oscar 🏮 prayed, "Father, you said that the prayer we pray in faith will save the sick. Melody is sick, very, very sick. Please touch her now and heal her, we pray, in Jesus's name. Amen."

🔭 James chapter 5 verse 15

Something amazing began to take place. Jesus rose up in Blazing Glory with healing in his wings. A bright light filled the sky and they could see a human outline form a canopy over where they had knelt to pray. The light wrapped itself around Melody. The Glides bowed their heads in awe and respect, unable to speak for they knew that God was present in a special way that day. Slowly the swelling went down and Melody sat up, ever thankful for the help and healing she had received. Right next to where she sat was a large green leaf which had fallen from one of the trees in the commotion. It had landed on her wound and covered the bite whilst the swelling went down. They all sat quietly for a time, not wanting to leave this seat of peace and healing that they had found.

🔭 Isaiah chapter 26 verse 3

Unfortunately, the Dupes were embroiled in the mud and commotion of Babylon. Stuck in the mud, with no peace or freedom to speak of, the lying lizard Wiz paid them a visit.

"Look, things can't get much worse can they? When it gets dark the bright lights of fun come on. You can get up to lots of mischief when it's dark and . . . not get caught. The old buzzard Vermont looks ancient and a bit worse for wear, so my advice to you is to just live it up a little," declared Wiz with a spell-binding glance. He specialized in using his long curling red tongue to reel others into his trap of lies.

"We have an early start tomorrow," responded Delilah, "and I have not got a thing to wear. My feathers are yesterday's news."

"Not to worry," lied Wiz, rolling his tongue like a magic wand. "When it's dark, who will know the difference?"

Jack thought on this a little. "If everyone goes out into the dark around here, then I can help myself to a bit of Babylonian treasure. Maybe even some valuable artefacts," Jack smirked to himself.

Dusk fell and the Glides watched the bright lights of the evening sky, considering why Father God should even bother to shine light for them. Devine said that Father God cared for each one of them personally.

Psalm 8 verses 3 & 4

They settled down to sleep for the night.

"I wonder what tomorrow will bring," sighed Penny.

"I think the troubles of today have been enough for all of us," chirped up Melody.

They all fell peacefully asleep under the watchful eyes of Devine. He found some large leaves that had fallen from the trees of life and laid them over each of them as a blanket.

The Dupes were restless and still awake.

Bored Charlie began to strip off some leaves from the hanging willows. "The night is only young," squawked Charlie. "And so am I. I need some life and action."

"Too young," Jack reminded him as he went off in a sulk.

"We're going to dance our claws away at the bird sanctuary. Babylonian Blues Brothers are playing tonight with Jazz Raven appearing later," said Delilah excitedly. "I'll soon be a teenager, so Charlie can stick with me."

"I'm off to make a few night calls," responded Jack. "So I'll see you here, back at the muddy river, at dawn."

Unfortunately, things did not turn out quite how they expected. Charlie got refused entry to the bird sanctuary as he was under age and looked it. So he spent the night comforting Delilah by the river of Babylon. Her feathers were not smart enough to get her in either. As for Jack, he was stalked by Jail Bird and arrested for breaking and entering into an upmarket golden cage in Babylon.

At dawn the Glides were up bright and breezy, ready for a new day.

Vermont came to wake his Dupes, only to find one missing and the other two stuck in the mud. Not that he cared a great deal. When he found out where Jack was he confiscated his bag of acquired tricks in payment of his bail. Jail Bird looked inside the bag and declared his belongings to be just a load of old rubbish, letting him keep his priceless treasures. With a long terrorizing glance from Vermont, Jail Bird agreed to let him go on one condition: that he stayed away from Babylon forever.

"A forever ASBO," cried Jack. "What will my mother say?" Jack was a mummy's boy really, although he had a hard exterior. He had got hooked on stealing when his dad had been locked up for life by Jail Bird. His mum could not afford much and so he stole to take care of the family.

Tired and miserable, the Dupes were not looking forward to another day. They knew that following Vermont was not all it appeared to be and it seemed that Vermont did not care either.

9

Peeling Patience

The morning filled the skies with bright hope for the Glides. Melody was an early bird who was glad to be alive. She had been changed by the trauma and rescue of yesterday. Being the first awake she was first to be touched by the following feather:

⚜ Jeremiah chapter 29 verse 11

"I wonder what Father's thoughts are of me today?" pondered Melody. Hope and exploding joy filled her heart as she read and she could not help but ring out a chorus or two.

"Sssshh," shouted Oscar, being disturbed from his sleep, "I can't hear."

"Let me sing louder then," said Melody pumping up the volume.

"No, silly, I can hear you all too clearly, but listen. What is that distant sound? I can hear bells ringing, peeling through the heavens."

With their beaks turned upwards towards the sky, Penny, now awake with all the commotion, joined them in wondering what all the excitement was about. They found the answer in their manuals:

Psalm 122 verse 1

"Time to go," hurried in Devine as Penny peeped over the top of Melody's shoulder to check out what the manual had to say.

"Go where?" wondered Penny curiously.

"Go to church. It's time to meet with other believers who will steer and encourage you on your journey," said Devine with a quiver of anticipation in his voice.

"But I won't know anyone, and I won't be able to see as I'm so little," whimpered frightened Penny.

"Won't, won't . . . what about can, can?" replied Oscar, irritated by his little friend.

"I can't, can't because I'm too shy and I don't know anyone there," replied Penny as the little butterflies continued to flutter about in her tummy. There was someone who could still her heart and the answer came, just like before, in the form of a simple white feather swirling to the ground to bring her the courage she needed:

Philippians chapter 4 verse 13

"There's nothing you can't do when you rely on Jesus to help you. He loves making people strong who feel weak. His strength is at its strongest when you let him help you," declared Devine. "Now, out with the ⊕ compass and on with the quest."

The compass spun around and pointed towards "life".

"There's no greater sign of life seen than when all of God's children get together as a big church. Just think of it as one big practice here on earth before the real thing in Blazing Glory," concluded Devine.

The Glides brushed down their feathers so that they were in their Sunday best. They took off, carried on the wings of worship, bouncing up and down to the sounds of the ringing bells. Melody and Penny held on tightly to Oscar and were on the lookout for a church steeple. The flight path was very quiet as it was Sunday morning. There was not a great deal of traffic in the skies as many ordinary birds were still tucked up in their nests. They gazed on the green grassy fields down below, where the dew remained undisturbed as the sun glistened on its tiny droplets.

Back in Babylon the Dupes were in a restless mood.

"Aaghh!" cried Charlie. "I've got beak ache. All this decay from this bag of treats has rotted the end of my beak."

"Tough!" snapped Vermont, in an uncaring way.

"Tough?!" shrieked back Charlie sharply. "I can't put up with this pain."

"Well you'll have to because all dentists are closed on Sundays," said Vermont biting back.

Rolling around in agony Charlie wailed, "What's more important, my aching beak or a day that has to be different? It can't be that special a day if it leaves me in pain." Charlie cried all the more, so much that all the Dupes developed a pounding headache.

Vermont was at the end of his feathers and could take no more. He decided to call in some favours and sent a letter by urgent pigeon carrier to someone he knew who dealt with tooth problems. In fact, it was someone who had a tooth problem herself, the toothless lion LuSINda. She was not that far away as she was on mission to stalk and bring down the Glides.

The pigeon flew in to collect the letter from Vermont. He looked a little strange as he had a wandering eye which would often cross over causing the pigeon to see double.

"That will be double time as it's Sunday," nodded the pie-eyed pigeon. Due to the squint in his eye the pigeon spent most of his time crashing into trees.

"Double time?!" yelled Vermont in a threatening tone. "You'll pay for this Charlie."

"Anything," pleaded Charlie in desperation. "You can take anything. I'll even sell you my soul. Just rescue me out of this pain."

So the muddy banks of Babylon became the waiting room for the next hour whilst the pie-eyed pigeon went in search of LuSINda.

Soaring high, the Glides were not looking back for anything. Straining towards the prize of Blazing Glory they went in search of a taste of what was to come. Intently looking for a large pointed steeple and a gathering of lots of people, Melody checked the ⊕ compass whilst she rested on Oscar's back. The compass spun around a few times in sheer excitement.

"What's going on here?" she asked Devine as the compass continued to spin.

"Ah yes, there are many ways God's people can come together. The Church, as they get ready to go home to Blazing Glory, meet in their communities. The Church isn't the steeple, the building or the place; it's the people. Now, let me see where we are on this tiny globe. If we take a sharp left then you will find Quality Street. The people who live there love wearing bright shiny wrappers for coats. Some of them are nice soft characters underneath their wrappings. Others may need a bit of work to get to know them – those hard centres just take a little more time to get through. It's a mixed bag and I have really got my work cut out, but Father loves them all. He is all-patient," explained Devine.

Oscar liked the sound of that assortment as he was growing up to be quite a cultured young bird. Soon to be on his way to senior school, the shiny wrappers grabbed his attention.

"If we take a right turn we can head down Celebration Alley. The people down there are a mixed packet of surprises who love to pull out all the stops when it comes to singing worship," said Devine getting rather excited.

"Oh happy day," scaled Melody. "That sure does flick all of my switches."

Penny went a little quiet at the thought of shiny wrappers since all she had was her common brown coat. Also, because she was a timid little girl she thought she probably wouldn't fit in with the noisy variety down Celebration Alley either.

Devine thought long and hard and hovered in the sky. "Maybe as we are passing through there is something different for you to see. The one common purpose that every one of God's children needs to unwrap and discover is found here. Follow me, straight ahead, to a group of believers who meet in the open pastures. This church has no walls since it's not about the building – the bricks are just the material that keeps everyone warm and together. The gospel, which is the great good news of Jesus, was always meant to GO – into every home, into every street, even to the farthest-most corner of the world," taught Devine. "All believers are to take the gospel out into the world." He pointed it out in the manual:

Mark chapter 16 verse 15

"Going into the whole world is a long-haul flight indeed and not for the faint-hearted," said Devine as he closed the manual.

Back in Babylon, Charlie was about to be painfully silenced. He had never thought he would be glad to see a dentist . . . but his joy was soon swallowed when he saw LuSINda. The lioness came pounding through the trees with her assistant Stavros, the saliva-dribbling fox. Stavros licked his lips at the sight of Charlie, which caused Delilah and Jack to fly up into the highest tree in a flap. They began to weep with the willows.

"What have we got here?" growled LuSINda.

As she smiled, all was revealed. She was a toothless, harmless cat really. Charlie quickly forgot his pain and joined the other Dupes up in the tree.

"Not much of an advert for being a good dentist," commented Jack, who could spot a con artist anywhere. LuSINda had lost her teeth from all the decay found in those bad tricks and treats. The rot had certainly taken its toll. Jack and Delilah gripped onto a strong branch of the tree with their long claws.

Charlie, exhausted from the pain, dropped his head in surrender. The moment he did was the moment he found unexpected help. He accidentally hit his beak onto the branch, just like a woodpecker. The offending piece of decay was broken from his beak and so Charlie was free of pain. With sheer bliss Charlie took off, well out of reach of LuSINda and Stavros. Charlie was happy to be free, and even happier to be getting away from the toothless cat and her dribbling assistant who ate birds like him for breakfast. Delilah and Jack were hot on his tail.

In all the commotion Vermont did an emergency take off, shouting, "If you think you can get away from me that easily, think again. Remember, you sold your soul Charlie, so you are mine!" shouted Vermont.

Seemingly snared for life, the Dupes slowed down to let Vermont take the fast current of air to gain the lead. They had all lost hope and could not even dare to believe that things could get better. And so they stayed on course to who knows where with Vermont.

Rippling through the valley, the sound of sweet music bounced off the hills. Straight in front of the Glides was a church gathering in open fields.

"Are we there yet?" Penny asked impatiently.

Oscar began to get ruffled under his feathers when Penny asked again, "How much further until we get there?"

"Pew," went Devine.

"Pew?" went the Glides.

"No I mean, pew, pew, sit in the pew," said Devine.

"What's a pew?" asked Melody, joining in on this crazy conversation.

"That bit of grass over there. It's where you can sit," explained Devine who had forgotten how infrequently his young students had been to church.

The field was a little crowded but Oscar found a patch of grass at the back of the gathering. Melody gave a long stretch with her wings and caught a whiff of something not too pleasant. She sniffed under her wing, and said, "Phew, I think I could do with the little birdies' room before I sit anywhere."

They all declared that she did and they would save her a blade of grass to come and sit on with them when she had finished washing and powdering her beak.

The church service went on a bit for little Penny. She began to be impatient and got fidgety feathers. Oscar got cross and told her to stop pecking and to listen to the Shepherd at the front. The Shepherd leant on a funny hooked stick and read from the same manual they had in their flight bags: the Bible. The Shepherd told them one of Jesus's famous tales about the hundred sheep and the one that went missing. Melody started counting, "One, two, three. . ."

"Don't count sheep," warned Oscar as she nodded off to sleep.

Luke chapter 15 verse 4 to 7

Whilst Oscar woke Melody for the final song, and Devine hovered over the whole congregation, Penny saw two large luminous eyes through holes in the hedge at the side of the field. One eye winked at her. Penny's interest was stirred and she fluttered over through the hole and out to the other side.

"Hello, what's your name?" asked the face attached to the eyes she had seen. Lured in by the friendly chatter, Penny felt flattered by the attention. In the darkness of the trees it was not clear who the stranger was. He seemed similar to the other people she had seen in the church. Closed in by the darkness, she felt a cold breeze and shivered with fear. A ray of light bounced off the dark creepy trees, like a flash from a camera.

Penny remembered the snapshots shown to her by Devine. Underneath his disguise of darkness was the Night Wolf. He had tricked Penny away from the safe pasture. Stunned by fear she did not know what to do. She thought up her quickest prayer ever. "HELP!" she cried in an undignified tone.

Devine, ever alert, heard the cry. He recognized Penny's voice. He never lost one who was in his care.

"I'm going to leave you here in these safe and open pastures," Devine said to Oscar and Melody. "Penny is in trouble. Please wait patiently."

"Patiently, what does that word mean?" asked Melody, who really didn't know what it meant to be patient.

"Just wait, expect good news, and don't move until I get back," said Devine as he took off on his mercy mission.

The Shepherd with the hooked stick, who seemed to understand what was happening, sent in Goodness and Mercy, his sheep dogs to help. Following the path of Devine, the good Shepherd was going to lend a helping hand too. Penny was hypnotized by the Night Wolf's eyes and could not move. She was surrounded by an army of tall dark trees. Seeing her paralyzed by fear, Devine sent a breeze to enable the others to be guided to the thicket where Penny was trapped.

Following the scent of the breeze, Goodness and Mercy pounced right in front of the Night Wolf and stared right back into his hateful gaze. Night Wolf could not bear to look for long into the truthful eyes of Goodness and Mercy, as the truth exposed his dark empty heart. His cover was blown by the daylight as the sheep dogs chased him away. The Good Shepherd, in hot pursuit of his sheep dogs, was not far behind. When he came to where Penny was he used his shepherd's hook to draw her to safety. He popped her up onto his shoulder and followed the wing-span of Devine back to the open pastures. The one that was lost had now been found.

There was a great celebration on their return. The Good Shepherd was really kind and threw a party of nuts and seeds. He took good care of his visitors. Before they left they wondered if they could make this church their home.

The Good Shepherd smiled and said, "For some it is right to stay here, but there are no walls because we want the gospel to go out into the world and not stay in just this one place. I will see you again in Blazing Glory. Now, may my grace and the love of the Father, along with the continuing guidance and friendship of the Holy Spirit, go with you, just as it remains here with us."

Devine led them away. It had been a full and patience-testing day. They found a quiet spot to rest, sat on some soft, spongy purple heather shrubs and made themselves comfortable.

Once they were settled, Devine began, "I think we should have an overdue visit to your 🍃 Hideaway. Look, the door is open into the 🐿 Eternal Fruit Garden. This fruit, patience, has definitely been tested today and I think you have all been left wanting."

"Wanting a drink!" declared thirsty Penny.

They all nestled in close and Devine looked at Penny, wondering if she was starting to understand her value. As one so small and young, she was taking some looking after. Still and quiet, they waited and waited and waited. Being good pupils they were starting to understand the value in waiting for something that was certainly worth waiting for. They were gently brushed with these words:

⚲ Isaiah chapter 40 verse 31

With their wings feeling stronger from the flights of the day, there was still more strength to come. An orange tree shone in the corner of the garden. The oranges were dazzling and bright. The feathered friends were all invited to take the fruit of patience.

"Why is this patient fruit?" they all asked.

They soon found out why when they tried to peel it! After a long-awaited drink of its juice they understood that the wait was worth it.

"There's never any disappointment to those who wait on God. You must patiently wait for him to show you his way," explained Devine.

⚲ Proverbs chapter 3 verses 5 & 6

Looking at these wise words they understood that taking short cuts and wandering off, going your own way, was not wise. It said so in this wise book of living words.

"Tweeta woo," agreed the wise owl, watching from the old oak tree. His big eyes provided the torchlight for Devine to sew the "patience" fruit onto their wings as the sun began to set in a glorious splash of orange in the sky.

⚲ Matthew chapter 7 verses 13 to 16

This feather of words dusted a chill of fear down the spines of the Glides, for they had come too close to the Night Wolf that day. They prayed for the patient nature of God to be embroidered onto their wings to guide them along the narrow way.

Devine left them with the following thought to puzzle over as they were rewarded with their badges. "Travel light," he said, "free to fly, free from sin, free from the fear of what others will think about you. Never be grounded."

Exhausted, they fell into a deep sleep, with the spongy purple heather mattress for a delightful nest.

10

A Kind Rooster or Two

Two kind roosters broke the silence of the morning. The Dupes, still feeling sore from the aches and pains of yesterday, didn't have a kind word on their beaks for the noisy roosters.

On the other hand, the Glides broke the morning's silence with a kind welcome to the day, and were tickled with this feather of words:

Psalm 18 verse 25

With the quest still unfolding they took to the wings of the morning. They sped eagerly in the direction the ✦ compass had turned to, down the "way". In fact, down a highway. It looked like they had a clear and smooth ride in store into enlarged borders and fruitful fields.

"What's all that hay-like stuff swaying in the breeze?" queried Penny.

"Ripe fields, ready for harvest," declared Devine excitedly.

"Wow, what a tasty crop. Can we hover around? There's bound to be plenty of field mice for the picking," piped up Oscar, with his tummy rumbling for breakfast.

"When is it time for harvest?" questioned Melody. She loved singing at the Harvest Festival assemblies.

"It's ripe and ready, just waiting for the command to harvest from Jesus, the Lord of the Harvest. His timing is perfect," smiled Devine.

As they drew a little closer, there was a flurry of traffic zooming past them in the opposite direction. They wondered what was going on and checked the ⊕ compass to see if the direction had changed. It still pointed forward. They knew that the kindness promised to them in Father's words that morning was waiting for them ahead, so they did not turn back like the other birds. Oscar had been looking over his shoulder instead of watching where he was going and suddenly there was a CRASH, THUD, BANG, WALLOP!

"What was that?" said Oscar, stunned. They looked up and saw this huge man-like straw figure. Trembling at the knees, Oscar started to speak out the following words from the manual.

Psalm 18 verse 29

"With your help I can attack an army. With God's help I can jump over a wall," quoted Oscar all in a dither.

Smiling under his beak Devine said, "I think you need to carry on with verse 30 . . . 'The ways of God are without fault, the Lord's words are pure.' The Father has not led you into danger. This is a scarecrow, quite friendly, in fact. Hop up onto his arms and we will take a breath or two and pray before we continue down the way."

With Babylon behind them and now just a distant nightmare, Vermont was driving the grumpy Dupes hard. He was never satisfied. He always demanded more and more but didn't give them anything other than tricks, treats and cheats. Nothing he gave them seemed to satisfy for long. Vermont was always most comfortable in the dark. There was a large black cloud ahead of them and he led the Dupes into it. It was a thick, dark rain cloud which rumbled as they entered. Piercing the darkness with their beaks, lightning cracked around them and the rain began to pour. Charlie tried to be brave, especially in front of Jack, but could not help giving out a squeal of terror. Their feathers became heavier and heavier with the downpour. They were forced to make an emergency landing, straight into a huge dark puddle. Shaking off the dirty water the Dupes were not amused. They spotted a disused hollow in a large oak tree and sheltered there until the rain stopped.

Delilah, in a rage, whirled her designer purse around and whopped Charlie on the head.

"What was that for?" asked Charlie, who was still embarrassed from squealing in front of Delilah.

"For nothing. Have that one on me. I just want to know when we are going to fly somewhere worth flying to," said Delilah.

Vermont gave one of his vile smiles. The evil genius was cooking up a plan. Spreading out his large black wings, he took off in a flash. The Dupes reluctantly followed. They ran as fast as they could to take off, just missing the large puddle they had crash landed in. Vermont turned a sharp right and headed towards a large tower. It looked grand. Much grander than anything they had ever stayed in before.

Jack asked, bellowing from behind, "What star rating does the tower have?"

"All stars that are worth their glitter stay at the Power Tower. It's the place to be seen," boasted Vermont, surging forward with his beak upturned with pride.

"Stars, stars," duplicated Charlie, "I'm going to touch beaks with a star!"

"Now you're talking my language," joined in Delilah. "But you must let me shop for something new. And, don't forget, I'll need a first class shampoo on my coat and my claws need painting. Look they're all chipped."

Jack wasn't too fussed about his feathers. All he could think about were the diamonds and pearls he might be able to steal while they were at the Power Tower. As they headed towards the city of Babel to its centre-piece Power Tower, their babblings became more selfish and unkind by the second. A cold mist rose from the ground as they got closer to the grey skies that dulled this wicked place.

Whilst the Glides paused for breath on the scarecrow's arm, Devine felt the strengthening breeze of a storm. Thick dark clouds were riding towards them. Sharply they took off and then dive-bombed towards a barn in the distance. The two kind roosters that had welcomed in the morning lived there and were delighted to take in some guests.

"How kind," said Penny, as she scurried in through a broken panel in the wooden barn.

They found themselves a warm rafter as they listened to the rain beginning to pound on the barn roof.

"Just in time," sighed Oscar with great relief. "I find it hard to fly when all my large feathers are wet."

"This makes a great Hideaway. Do you think we will be able to find the Eternal Fruit Garden here?" questioned Penny.

"What's that?" asked Clarence the rooster.

Clarence had regal feathers that fanned out of his head. He had six in all.

"Can we come too?" joined in his identical twin Doodle.

Doodle's feathered crown fanned in the other direction, which helped everyone know who was who.

Penny suddenly felt lost in a bigger crowd and turned them down quite harshly. "No, you can't come. You're not one of us!"

"Penny," said Devine. "That wasn't kind."

"Well, there may not be enough of all this good fruit to go around and besides, any more than three is crowded," moaned Penny. Her ugly tone now matched her common brown feathers.

"There's more than enough for everyone in Blazing Glory," said Devine, bringing the needed correction to Penny's words:

🔭 Romans chapter 10 verse 13

"So, do you see there is enough for everyone now, Penny?" Devine asked. "Clarence and Doodle have asked if they can know the Father too. He has no favourites, and doesn't mind whether we look the same or not," said Devine gently.

"Sorry," said Penny, her cheeks turning a bright shade of red.

So they made the circle larger and sat quietly, 🔭 waiting and listening to God.

Devine fluttered the tips of his wings to turn the pages of the Bible, and found a true story to inspire the seekers:

🔭 John chapter 6 verses 5 to 14

"Stare into this little boy's lunch box," Devine challenged the Glides. "One, two, three, four, five loaves and two fish times five thousand mouths to feed. Hmmm," Devine's eyes glanced around the birds and landed on Oscar. "Oscar, is that possible to do, as well as have twelve baskets left over?"

Oscar enjoyed a mathematical challenge but this left even his brain in a whirl. He could not work it out. Even if they only had as much as a crumb each, there still would not be enough.

"Impossible!" declared Oscar.

"Impossible for man, but with God all things are possible," laughed Devine.

"It was kind of the boy to share," piped up Penny.

"Well observed my young friend," encouraged Devine.

Opening the fruit of kindness, which was a pomegranate, they all took turns in extracting one of its sweet pink seeds with their beaks. As they enjoyed the fruit Devine continued with his lesson.

"Father made more than enough of everything for it to be shared amongst everyone. It's only as you are kind and share that there is enough to go around and with plenty left over if you are not greedy. When you give something out of kindness to someone, you are giving to the Father. He cannot help being generous because his nature is to be kind. It does not matter how small a thing you give to the Father – even one kind word to someone else is enough to fill a heart with lots of kindness to last them a day. The miracle that grows from your kind action is in the hands of the Father and he will bless what is given."

With sticky wing tips, they all had the fruit of kindness badge attached onto their wings. Penny spread her wings to make room for her next badge. The twin roosters could not help but admire the mass display of colour decorating the tiny sparrow's wings.

"My, oh my, we love your beautiful coat. Where did all that fruitful colour come from?" asked Clarence with a longing look.

Devine gave a word of kindness to Clarence and Doodle: "Just as you two twins look like each other, so as you get to know the Father God for yourself, you become like him. When the Glides wrap their wings around someone that needs help, others will see it and praise the Father, because they are behaving like him."

The storm died down and Devine promised to be with Clarence and Doodle too. He gave them each a flight pack containing a Bible and compass and promised he would guide them down the way to Blazing Glory. For now, the twins waved the Glides goodbye with their Mohican head feathers. Flying into a sky painted with a rainbow of promise, the Glides wondered what treasure lay in store on their exciting journey.

The twists and turns of a bumpy flight had taken the Dupes to a dead-end dark alley, but this hadn't grabbed their attention. What had captured their gaze were the bright lights and loud music of Babel.

"This Power Tower was built for the glory of all creatures. It is a demonstration of the kind of determination and application that brings notable and applauded success," boasted Vermont with big words matching his even bigger head. "In fact," proclaimed Vermont, with his chest sticking out with pride, "I was the original architect. The name 'Evil Genius' is something I have worked tirelessly on, ever since I moved kingdoms. You see, I used to live in Blazing Glory but I couldn't stand all that light. Light is no good as far as I am concerned . . . unless the spotlight is on ME, of course."

"Tell us more," swooned Delilah, bewitched by his momentary spell of power.

"Father, the great 'I AM', as he likes to be known, didn't appreciate my new style of music. I wrote my own lyrics all about myself and not about him. I was the best composer and all-round musician in the kingdom of Blazing Glory and, might I add, with a certain amount of beauty and obvious charm," boasted Vermont. "I had some of the wing-flapping angels enchanted. In fact, so enchanted that we were all shown the door and sent here, for what seems like an eternity. Well, I don't rate Blazing Glory anyhow. It's all too pure and right. My dark side was not welcome there. You see, there is no darkness there at all."

Jack thought twice about whether Blazing Glory would suit him. There would be nowhere to hide things when he stole them. The other two felt overcome with a dark chill and thought they had heard enough of the dark tale for one day.

Turning their attention away from the tale they stared at the tower. It was tall and a dark shade of grey. The moon lit up its commanding height like a huge spotlight where bats liked to flap around as if on stage. Quickly they checked into the Power Tower and got their beaks ready for a trilling five star meal.

11
Land of the Giants

The Dupes were served the most gigantic plate of bird seed they had ever feasted their eyes upon, and that was just the first course. By the end of the night their eyes bulged nearly as big as their bellies. Nursing the worst tummy aches ever, they retired to their king-sized nest in the penthouse suite at the top of the Power Tower. This was Vermont's very own apartment. They were all so fat from their meal that they rode the lift separately as a precaution. Delilah decided not to hit the Tower dance floor that evening, and not just because she might break it after all that grub. It was more due to the fact that she could not fasten her new designer belt.

As they entered the penthouse it took their breath away. It was a nest above all other nests. Each twig had been lined with pure gold and stuffed with the finest duck feathers. The Dupes could not believe their lucky beaks. They crossed their claws, hoping their good fortune would not run out too soon and then made themselves comfortable.

The Glides had a completely different evening in store. It would be far from comfortable, in fact, it would be very dangerous. Devine instructed them that they would take a night flight, as they were going to fly through enemy airspace.

Some areas had been given over to dark enemy activity. Vermont's chief commander, Beelzebub, was in charge of a crack squad of buzzards. With feathers as black as soot, the buzzards were large, mean and ready for war.

If any Blazing Glory pathfinders wanted to pass through their airspace, they had better be prepared for battle. Devine had told them that all those who are on the path to Blazing Glory have enemies because they are part of God's kingdom. God's kingdom has always suffered at the hands of its enemies, so those wanting to see great things happen have to be prepared for a battle. The Glides read from their manuals and dressed themselves for battle:

Ephesians chapter 6 verses 11 to 18

Devine drilled them on their upcoming armoured flight. He taught them how to defend and to advance as they passed through enemy territory.

"Watch out," he said, "and keep ☄ praying. There will be tricky words which will try to bring you down that you must get through. Don't be afraid, no matter what the light shines on in the darkness."

The Glides broke into a scared sweat, but a feather came down with words to wipe away their fear:

Psalm 56 verses 3 & 4

"Keep God's praise on your beaks. This will ensure you stay out of the enemies' reach. Always remember the promise of Blazing Glory, for your hope is certain and your protection guaranteed," reassured Devine. Devine then quoted from the manual, promising, "If you follow this next verse you will most certainly be rewarded with a forever prize in Blazing Glory."

Romans chapter 8 verse 18

Oscar opened his manual to the page that Devine had read from. It shone a bright light into the darkness so that they could see their way in the black night sky and on to victory. With a thrust of faith and a believing expectancy they continued forward on their journey.

Flying like three true agents of God's kingdom they spied out the land beneath. The manual worked like a huge spotlight on what was happening on the ground.

"Look at the size of those!" squealed Penny.

"The size of whose nose?" asked Melody.

"No, no, no, the size of those, those . . . GIANTS," said Penny in a state of panic, catching sight of the buzzards.

Oscar took a nose-dive towards the ground at the warning about giants. Devine sped from behind to their rescue, lifting them with the words, "Beaks upwards. Remember 'in God whose words I praise'. This will take you out of enemy fire."

The buzzards spotted the Glide formation flying high above; flying so high above that they couldn't hope to reach them. They began to fire words of doubt at them to bring them down.

"Don't think you can escape us," the buzzards yelled, trying to terrify them with their words.

"We're going to get you."

"There's no way you can make it."

"Blazing Glory is too far away. Come down here and stay with us for a while."

"Your friends are having a great time down here. They love it."

"Come and have some fun!"

"You must be lonely up there with only three of you."

The words seemed to rattle through the air like a machine gun.

The Glides dodged the words of doubt and fear that had tried to bring them down. Safe in the current of high praise, Melody kept them in good voice. Devine sent quiet words through the airwaves to encourage their hearts. The stars seemed to blink in the sky, like a large crowd of eyes watching the fight. "Maybe the angels are having a peep," thought Penny, holding on tightly.

Then Devine spoke to give greater confidence to the Glides. "A land full of promise awaits you. Imagine free milk to drink, honey, and grapes; everything you could ever hope for but it won't come easy. Speeding through the sound barrier won't win the day. Be steady in trusting God each day. Remember, Jesus gave you the ultimate flight path as he targeted himself, like a sharp arrow, towards his given quest. He didn't look down. He didn't look back. His mission to the cross was filled with suffering but what was won was so great that its value is still being counted as the flight to Blazing Glory continues for those who will come. Jesus's mission was very costly because he laid down his life for others. We too need to put others' needs before our own. You have to do what Father wants you to do rather than selfish things for yourself. That's what it means to lay down your life. That's what Jesus did."

It all got a bit emotional for Melody, who hit a low note and tumbled off Oscar's wing. It was so dark they could not see where she had fallen. She tumbled through the darkness and with a painful thud hit the ground. Melody lay with her armour strewn all over the floor. Bruised and in a daze she crawled to hide under the nearest bush. With her flight bag still hooked to her wing she opened the pages at:

🔭 Psalm 27

This was a long read, but so was her wait. She left the pages open as the words made her warm and unafraid. As she did they brought light into her darkness like a night lamp. The light shone an SOS into the dark night sky. Seeing the flash of light piercing the dark sky the Glides made an emergency landing on a pebbled path. The path led into the forest of trees where the buzzards had nested and made their base camp.

Quietly, as the buzzards were on full alert, the Glides searched the ground in their full armour. They found Melody's helmet, sword and shield abandoned nearby on the floor. They quickly picked them up in case they fell into enemy hands.

"At least she has the breastplate of righteousness on, held tight by the belt of truth," said Oscar, running through the checklist of armour from his manual.

"What about her shoes? Do you think Melody still remembers that she can walk in peace even if she is surrounded by fear?" said Penny with a caring sigh.

"No true follower ever forgets their good news shoes so that they are always ready to tell others about the way," explained Devine.

"Keeping watch throughout the night is a hard thing," said Oscar. "Especially when you can't see what is happening." He began to worry about Melody. Oscar could sense that the buzzards were too close for comfort.

Devine smiled and said, "Perhaps when the curtains of the sky are closed in darkness, it just means that God is getting something greater ready for the morning, when they are drawn back with light. Remember, this sorrow may last the night but joy always comes in the morning. These are words of promise which have never failed, and never will. Hope and trust in God."

The night was long for Melody but even longer for the Dupes who had awful belly ache. Charlie ate the most as his eyes were far bigger than his belly. His tummy ache was the worst and rumbled the loudest. The penthouse suite may have been fine and dandy but did not bring the comfort needed when you need your mother.

"I want my mum," moaned Charlie, over and over again.

"Quiet, Charlie," insisted Jack. "No one can help you here. I did a quick scout around and all I could hear were others babbling in strange languages. No one seems to understand each other and everyone is very confused. There is no help to be found in Babel."

Delilah looked at them both. "That's what you get when a power surge happens. Everyone thinks they are right and that they are the most important. Power should be used for the good of others otherwise it becomes destructive," remarked Delilah.

"My, my, my, Delilah," interrupted inquisitive Vermont. His beak was electrified with tension and shone like a beacon.

Delilah quickly closed her beak and hung her head in despair.

They were ordered out of their room even before the sun came up. Their good fortune did not even last the full night. Empty of hope and longing to be loved, they left Babel totally confused and overweight. They were so heavy they could only fly very low with their tummies scraping the ground.

"Get me out of this God-forsaken country," cried Charlie, in greater need of his mother. "I want to go home!"

Snared by the angry fowler, Vermont, they felt completely trapped.

"For goodness sake!" shouted Vermont. "I can't wait until I can drop you three at lost baggage. Maybe at the next runway," he muttered to himself.

"Runway, I think *run away* would be better," agreed the Dupes, whispering behind Vermont's back.

The sun was still not ready to rise and the night dragged on. With her light under a bush, Melody was hard to find. She needed some outside help and with that thought a feather was blown under the bush:

Matthew chapter 5 verses 14 & 15

As soon as Melody had read the words she cried, "That's it, I must not hide the light!" She pushed her Bible out from under the leaves. This courageous act brought its reward:

Matthew chapter 5 verse 16

At once, help came to Melody. Devine and the other Glides, who were still searching hard, saw it and flew to the light. Many others also loved living in the light too. All varieties of feathered friends were drawn to it: red, yellow, and blue. They were all amazed at how God had kept Melody safe and unharmed in such a dangerous place. Together they talked about the Father's Blazing Glory and the Father heard them:

 ## Malachi chapter 3 verse 16

Melody's joy suddenly became an anxious thought and she asked, "Won't the buzzards see the light?"

"Don't be afraid," replied Devine. "Most of the time they cannot bear to see the light at all, it makes them want to hide."

Devine blessed them all with the tip of his wing, leading them into the Eternal Fruit Garden. Here they were hidden in the promise of all that God had prepared for them even though they had touched down in the Land of the Giants.

An enormous melon was rolled from down the way. It came thundering across the large green lawn in the fruit garden. Their eyes popped out with amazement and pleasure as they all had a feast on God's goodness to them. Father's heart is massive, bigger than the largest melon. There were many who had not tasted this goodness before, so they took their first bite of knowing Father for themselves. Devine had quite a number of melon badges to sew on that day,

"Goodness me," he whispered as he stitched the goodness of the Father onto each wing ready to fly carrying the mark of his nature.

Penny was asked to read out a closing thought to them all – quite a big challenge for a shy little girl but with God's help it was not a problem:

🔭 Psalm 133

Meanwhile, the giant buzzards raged around the skies, looking out for a tasty spread of fallen flyers. They buzzed in fury. There were no victims to be found in the Land of the Giants this day. Beelzebub was furious at the failure of his flight squad and threatened to cast them even further into outer darkness if they did not stop all flights to Blazing Glory.

"How did they manage to get through?" buzzed the buzzards, who never took defeat kindly and who lived in dread of Beelzebub.

Bully Bear stomped around too, expecting to find a weak victim to torment. He was still not giving up on bringing down the Glides either.

"What is going on? This is our patch and they're getting too close to seeing the promise fulfilled," growled Bully Bear in a rage.

As the sun rose with a wing-span of blazing light, the Glides took off, victorious. They were strong and courageous students and they left the Land of the Giants under the cover of light. Nothing could penetrate God's power to keep them safe. In the 🌪 eye of his peace their faith increased.

This was preparing them for great exploits, just like the many heroes who had gone before them. And all because they were getting to know the Father and what he is like.

🔭 James chapter 1 verse 17

12
Faithful Friend

Getting into Babel was easy but getting out of this powerful city was a nightmare. It seemed to take all day. The Dupes, with bellies still bulging and touching the ground, got stuck in a heaving crowd. They could not fly above the crowd because of their eating binge. And besides, they could not take off because there was no long clear runway. The crowd could not walk straight and nearly crushed young Delilah.

The people all seemed to be singing the same song, "You'll never walk alone". This was the favourite hymn of the local football fans. Babel United, with all the money and power, had of course won again. The words of the song seemed to add salt to the wounds of homesick Charlie. He wondered why in such a large crowd he could still feel so alone.

Charlie desperately longed for Vermont to play a good card into the hand of misfortune dealt to them on this quest. The bag of tricks and treats seemed to have a hole in it. Nothing seemed to satisfy the longing inside. The empty bag feeling they were all carrying around just got worse and worse. The city was meant to be the place where everything was happening. It seemed to be happening all around, but not for them. The only good thing, they thought, was the bits of bread dropping to the ground from the football fans' burger rolls, which they readily ate.

"Why am I eating these crumbs when I'm already full?" thought Jack.

Quite unexpectedly, a glimmer of hope seemed to flutter from the sky. A feather flew down:

◖ Isaiah chapter 55 verse 6

Charlie caught it in his beak and hid it in his bag of tricks and treats. "If only I had brought my manual I could find out what these words are saying to me," thought Charlie. His heart warmed a little as the feather had given him a small spark of life.

Happily for Charlie, Vermont missed the falling feather as something else had caught his mean eye. A lamp in a window down Main Street grabbed his attention. "Dupes, there's a little information I need to gather before we continue on our journey. You go and wait in the old churchyard just over the road," said quick-thinking Vermont. Usually he would have kept them away from churchyards but everything in this one was long dead. "I'll send Stavros, the dribbling fox, to you to watch out that you're okay. He's got a fine bushy tail and will be able to keep you amused with his stories," said Vermont in a disinterested tone.

Very much afraid, their beaks dropped. Exhausted, they flew to the bench by the church door, away from the crowded street. The churchyard was deserted. It was late in the afternoon and the setting sun cast its shadow across the moss-covered gravestones. The Dupes didn't speak but held their breath listening to every whisper the trees made as the breeze swayed their branches. Stunned and still, they looked out for Stavros, hoping his stories would take their minds off the scary scene.

Vermont licked his coat of feathers, tucked in his tail and flew to the apartment window, singing "Polly put the kettle on".

Polly, a gorgeous female parrot, was his feathered friend. She wore a stunning pink feather boa. She would warm Vermont's dark feathers by filling him in on all the local gossip. How long he would leave the Dupes waiting was anyone's guess. Charlie just peeped inside his bag of tricks and treats to look at the feather of hope. He secretly longed, even prayed, things would soon change for the better.

The Glides left the Land of the Giants as victorious soldiers with a huge new-found feathered family. They had landed in all that had been promised to them by Father's words.

The giant buzzards had been driven into hiding by the light, hungry and downcast. The large flock of birds flew over a bright and colourful landscape. They hopped from tree to tree to sample the sticky honey running from the honeycombs. The sugary taste gave them a surge of life to energize them for their continuing flight to Blazing Glory.

Feeling a bit thirsty, Oscar noticed some hairy coconuts which had dropped from a tree and lay open on the ground. He swiftly landed with Melody and Penny for a long drink of the coconut milk. Their new friends soon joined them. Things had never looked so good. They laughed as they talked together about how in reality the giants only looked like grasshoppers compared to the size of their great God. Their expectation for the future had grown bigger than their imagination.

They played joyfully with their new friends. The Glides tried to race a flock of swifts but they couldn't keep up with the darting birds. Down below, Oscar spotted a deep gorge. They bombed down into the gorge and Penny squealed with delight. As the gorge took a shallow turn they came face to face with a high mountain. It looked stunning, so strong and mysterious. A large cloud hung low over the top of its snowy peak, and a peaceful heaviness caused them to land at its base.

"Where are we?" wondered Oscar, lost for words.

"This is Mount Sonyi, a place where the voice of God can be powerfully heard," explained Devine. He had seen the Glides' every move and followed them at a safe distance.

Held back by a respectful fear, no one dared to move. They became as still as statues. Devine told them how those who climbed the mountain came back different, as if a ray of the "blaze" had dusted their faces.

"Who can even climb this mountain? Can anyone ever be good enough?" said Penny as she tucked herself behind tall Oscar.

In answer, a pure feather fluttered down and balanced at Penny's feet:

Psalm 24

As they looked up, the words of this psalm blew down from the mountain on pure white feathers, each word lining the path like snow inviting them to walk up. The tips of their wings were miraculously dusted with a silver lining, for they were being made ready to climb. As they climbed high everything else paled into insignificance.

Sitting on a high ridge, something heavy and yet so light rested on their heads as Father's wing over-shadowed them, reassuring them of how kind and loving he is. They were familiar with the ♡ Hideaway but today would be different, a special day, which made them feel honoured to be part of this amazing event. Slowly, a door to the 🌺 Eternal Fruit Garden opened and a ripe mango appeared before their eyes.

"This is the fruit of 'faithfulness'. It is for you to eat and know that your Father can be trusted as a faithful friend. You will receive your usual fruit badge but there is something more for you, as you have shown by your hearts that you are true family friends. When you draw near to God he will draw near to you. He only tells his secrets to his true friends."

Devine peeled the mango and they all devoured its sweet perfumed orange pulp. As they pecked deeper into the mango, they found something hard in the middle. It was a crinkled stone. Oscar's long beak was the first to touch it.

"What is that?" he squawked.

"It's a stone in the heart of the fruit. This is how your heart is before you become a true and faithful friend of God. Right at your centre is a hard heart that always wants its own way. For true faith to work, that hard stone has to be removed," instructed Devine.

Melody swooned at the thought of being asked to have her hard heart taken out. As she lay semi-awake on the ground, Devine reassured her, "This is what Father does for his true friends. How can you truly carry his heart if your hard one gets in the way?"

"But I don't want you to take out my heart. And his heart is too big to fit in my little body. What about all the blood?" said Penny feeling a little concerned.

Devine swapped her fears with these words as he said, "Father doesn't mean your beating heart. He means that he wants to change all your wrong thoughts, wrong attitudes and wrong behaviour and replace them with his thoughts and actions. This is what he means by giving you a new heart."

They then opened the pages of their Bibles and found out just what would happen:

Ezekiel chapter 36 verses 26 & 27

Each Glide waited and prayed for a heart like God's heart. After a time of waiting, the three Glides got up and came down the mountain with their wings around each other, ready for any new challenge the journey might bring.

"Friends of a feather will stick together," they all chirped. With loyal hearts for Father and towards each other, no mountain could ever stand in their way.

Lurking at the foot of the mountain, unable to climb up was Bully Bear. With fearless hearts the Glides knew they were free and untouchable. They knew their God would not fail them even when big bullies get in their way. Full of faith, they were not snared by the fowler's trap. They flew above the tip of the angry bully's claw. Oscar even showed off with a couple of his loop de la hoops, just to frustrate Bully Bear's nasty plan.

Suddenly, a beautiful red ruby dazzled their eyes. It shone above them like a star. It was the Glides' chance to gain this valuable jewel.

"Do you want to gain this treasure," Devine whispered, "so that it will be stored for you in Blazing Glory?"

"Looks costly," said Melody. "But I'm sure it will be worth it."

Devine went on, pointing out the manual's instruction, "This is your mission and it is what you have to do to prove to be faithful friends."

 Proverbs chapter 18 verse 24

"Now my friends," said Devine. "There has been an SOS delivered to me on the secret winds from one of the Dupes, cheeky Charlie. He is in desperate need. His prayer has been heard and I need help from those who know how to be faithful friends."

Ready and prepared, like good Glides, Penny got out the ⊕ compass and shouted to the others, "Which way for the mission?"

The compass spun around to the "way", pointing them to follow their new hearts to help a friend in need.

Wasting no time, Oscar rose high above the clouds to take an express current, with Penny and Melody clutching the feathers on his back.

"Look out for the Power Tower and stay prayerful as you enter this danger zone," warned Devine. "You must remain in the 🌀 eye of Father's peace. Babel is full of chaos and distraction."

Melody then managed to catch a flying feather in her beak and read it to the others:

🖋 Matthew chapter 5 verse 9

Still waiting in the dark deserted churchyard, Charlie was now all alone. His other friends had long since deserted him.

Vermont had finished with the Dupes and had abandoned them to a life in the lost city of confusion. Vermont knew there was no one around in this city to direct them in the right way. There was no way out for them. Vermont had gone in search of new young fledglings to trick and treat down a dead-end road.

Jack had been caught stealing and, with a criminal record already, was taken into a cage by Jail Bird. Waiting on "Bird Row", his sentence was yet to be decided.

Delilah had gone shopping to jolly up her feathers. She thought she was too well dressed to come back to a church-yard. With her new image she had found a new group of friends in Babel.

All alone, Charlie just talked to himself, holding onto his feather of hope. Stavros the saliva-dripping fox hung around to revel in the misery, taunting, "Oh dear, haven't you got a friend in the world Charlie? Never mind, pet. Maybe someone will take pity on you and find you a perch to swing on in the Power Tower."

The Glides flew through the night, on the secret winds which would take them straight to Charlie. As the sun rose, the Glides and Devine flew in formation on the wings of the morning, united as one, to bring Father's help to Charlie. As the Glides came closer, Stavros' mouth dried up in an instant and silenced his lies and taunting. He tucked his bushy tail between his legs and scurried off. Stavros was brave when he had a helpless, hopeless victim to taunt. But when he saw, in the distant morning sky, bright lights in close formation approaching rapidly, he panicked and ran. He remembered that he had been defeated and beaten so many times before by creatures carrying that same bright light.

"Hello friend," said Penny to Charlie as they landed in the churchyard.

Charlie looked twice over his shoulder as he had not heard the word "friend" used in such a long time. Oscar, peering over his glasses, repeated the greeting as Charlie liked to hear words repeated. Charlie began to cry, stopped, then cried again.

"I'm lost and alone. No one can point me to the way. I didn't bring my Bible and compass and so all I could do was pray. I didn't expect an answer as I have done so many wrong things," Charlie declared with tears pouring off the end of his beak like a waterfall.

"Are you ready to turn around and go the right way?" asked Devine.

"If only I could, but I don't know how," answered Charlie.

They all put their fruit feathers around him and helped him see from their manuals:

Philippians chapter 3 verses 13 & 14

"There is a prize up there to win? I've not heard that one before. Do you think I can win it?" asked Charlie as a feather brushed him on the shoulder in answer to his question:

2 Corinthians chapter 5 verse 17

Oscar speedily looked up these words for Charlie in his manual, and then they ⬧ prayed with Charlie.

Charlie felt brand new and clean. For the first time in a long time he felt free and ready to fly. Devine gave him directions to a new "Camp of Life" to start him on his new journey of faith to Blazing Glory. Devine promised to meet him there.

Devine prepared for them a light lunch of bread and red berry juice. They had a special time to remember what Jesus had done for them in making their flight possible. Melody could not resist the opportunity to sing, and as Charlie had not heard her before he kept asking for a repeat. Not sure how many more repeats Oscar could bear, each of the birds gave Charlie a friendship wing-hug before he left.

Charlie flew off with his bright red tail electrified by the change, ready to start a new chapter on his own personal journey to Blazing Glory. As you would expect, his gift of the gab to talk to others was unstoppable. He told all who he flew past of his new friendship and, like a magnet, attracted them in the direction of Blazing Glory.

13
Gentle Touch

Hearing the gentle breeze in the tops of the mulberry trees, Devine turned his attention away from the excitement of the Glides as they played in the afternoon sun.

"What's happening?" Melody gently enquired.

"It's the sound of Father moving things in the skies and it's time to go."

Penny quickly pulled out the ⊕ compass and it span around towards "life". Before she had a chance to comment Devine took flight. In a hurry, Melody and Penny climbed up onto Oscar's back and followed after Devine. They all wondered why he had moved from behind their tail to lead the way. Great enthusiasm bubbled up inside them in the slipstream of Devine's tail. The breeze combed through their feathers.

The Glides were captured by the strange sight in the sky. Flocks of birds from the north, south, east and west were migrating in the same direction. It seemed as if something had changed and a message was being carried on the secret winds. There was urgency in their flight. Carried along in the flow, they became aware of how late it was. Approaching darkness seemed to colour the sky with a brush of watercolour paint; just as if Heaven was weeping. In the distance a bright light shimmered like a sea of glass. A loving deep voice called out across the empty space and echoed through the sky. They drew ever closer to the sound. Behind them peeled distant rolls of thunder and crashes of light lit up the sky from where they had flown.

The distant skyline held the most amazing sunset the Glides had ever seen. It was a masterpiece. It seemed to them like the sun was setting on the old, and yet at the same time dawning on a new beginning. Suddenly, a whirlwind carried them up higher than they had ever flown before and they touched down on a bright white cloud. With a bird's-eye view they scanned this glorious sight. This was a 🖤 Hideaway above all others, where their last-but-one fruit was to be tasted. In the 🌸 Eternal Fruit Garden they gazed on the funniest-looking fruit ever created. It was green and hairy and tickled their beaks.

"What's that?" asked Melody.

Oscar responded in a posh tone, "A kiwi fruit."

Penny loved the little pips that popped with a refreshing ping inside her beak.

🔭 Psalm 18 verse 35

They understood God's power but were in awe of his gentle nature.

Devine embroidered the fruit of gentleness onto their wings. They could hardly feel the pull of the thread.

"How can such a strong God touch us in such a gentle way?" responded Oscar, with a lump in his throat.

They looked around them and were amazed beyond their wildest dreams. On each of the fluffy white clouds were ancient birds. These were the many birds of faith mentioned in their Bibles, the heroic birds from the past who had already successfully followed the way to Blazing Glory:

Hebrews chapter 12 verses 1 & 2

They sang about heroic tales of old. They were cheering the Glides on to go and win the prize too. Penny, Oscar and Melody looked up higher. On the highest cloud they could see what looked like the Master.

"It's him," they cried. "It's Jesus!"

Devine raised his pure white wings over them and said, "The hour is late and there is much for you to do. *Blazing Glory is coming*. Before you can complete your journey there is one final task prepared for each of you in order to finish. And in order to do this, you must always keep your eyes on Jesus."

Devine saw the puzzled looks on their faces and so explained what this meant.

"This means reading about him in your manual, understanding what he would do and always talking with him in your Hideaway. He has begun an epic tale in each of your lives and he will finish the story. Jesus will fill each page of your days with wonders and his miracles. He will make everything perfect in his time. Look into his face."

They all stared intently and fixed their eyes on Jesus.

"Read the good news. He is calling as many as will come to Blazing Glory and there is not much time left," said Devine.

A large clear blue teardrop fell from heaven and crystallized on their cloud.

"This jewel is the most beautiful and costly. It is won as you obey Jesus's final words spoken on earth," said Devine. The friends looked up the words in their manuals and Devine taught them what he meant:

Matthew chapter 28 verses 18 to 20

Carrying these words deep in their hearts they came down gently from the cloud, ready to go and take the gospel – the good news about God and Jesus – to wherever they were to be sent.

14

Selfless Flying

The Glides made an emergency landing, just avoiding a pineapple tree.

"Pile up!" shouted Melody as they all landed on Oscar's soft belly.

The thud caused a pineapple to fall and hit Melody on the head.

"That'll teach you," laughed Oscar.

His belly wobbled like a big bowl of jelly as they tumbled off and onto the ground.

They were still in the 🍇 Eternal Fruit Garden. The final tutti frutti to dress their wings with the Father's nature had landed. "This is your final fruit. Then you will be fully clothed," declared Devine.

"It's a bit prickly," said Penny touching the top of the pineapple, "but I do like the spiky hairdo."

"Father loves variety," smiled Devine. "He likes you to be yourself because he created each of you to be especially unique." The pineapple skin was tough to break through. Devine sliced it with his beak. "There's so much good inside everyone. Sometimes, getting past the hard exterior is the biggest problem. That sweet nature is there to be shared.

Sometimes you don't let others close. You keep yourself to yourself. This isn't how it's meant to be," instructed Devine, looking at them with his piercing blue eyes. It seemed as if he was reading their thoughts. "If you're going to go into all parts of the world as carriers of the gospel one day soon, you'll have to be selfless like Jesus." With bits of yellow pineapple still in his beak he opened the pages of his manual for them to read:

Philippians chapter 2 verses 5 to 11

With that, the Glides shared the pineapple around. Oscar took a really large piece and squeezed it into juice for them all to enjoy. Melody thought she'd make the top into a crown for

Oscar. She wanted to see how he'd look one day when he got his real crown in Blazing Glory.

"Oscar the overcomer!" she declared placing the crown on his head, using her beak to blow a trumpet blast.

Oscar laid the pineapple crown on the ground as the fruit badge of "self control" was sewn onto each of their wings.

Devine responded, "Jesus laid down his crown just like that so that you could come into his kingdom. The King had to come so that you could find the way."

Sipping on the juice of the pineapple, they swallowed hard when they read this verse:

John chapter 14 verse 6

"The time has come for you to go into the world, where the Father has already prepared good things for you to do. You look so amazingly like him now, with your colourful coats. Before you go I have some gifts for you. Use the gifts wisely in order to become everything the Father wants you to be and to grow more like him," chuckled Devine with excitement.

"Gifts," squealed Penny with delight. "I've never had a gift before. What should I do with mine?"

"Open it, that would be a good start," smiled Oscar.

Ripping off the paper, they each received their own special gift.

"They are yours for keeps, to use selflessly for others. You need self-control in order to use your gifts well. If your gifts are admired by others, make sure you cover them with your wings. Tell them the gifts were given to you by the Father. Give Father the praise you receive, rather than accepting it for yourselves. The gifts are given to you so that others will see the Father and come to know him," instructed Devine, with stern caution.

"How do we know what to do with the gift?" asked Oscar.

"Follow the manual, your Bible. It is full of all the help you need. Pray and ask for wisdom when you need it, and listen for my whisper and I will guide you through," said Devine. "Your wings have been decorated so that you hold your gift in the right way. Don't misuse it or bury it, but invest it in things that last forever."

And so it was that each Glide flew onwards and upwards. They were fully equipped for an extraordinary life. Devine twisted his tail to turn and find newcomers looking for the way to Blazing Glory. He was also ever present with the Glides. They left the garden, full and free to follow the rest of their trail to Blazing Glory. With adventure and miracles in store, and ever watchful, the Glides never forgot to daily find their Hideaway. This would forever remain their favourite place to spend time with their very best friend.

Psalm 91 verses 1 & 2

GO FLY!

www.blazing-glory.com

Hi there!

If you want to know even more about Blazing Glory and follow new adventures every week, then go to the Blazing Glory website www.blazing-glory.com which is live from 31 October 2008.

Meet all the characters and enjoy new journeys on the way to Blazing Glory as you discover words of wisdom and stories of faith, courage, hope and love.

Many of you will want to start out on your own journey of adventure to Blazing Glory. Every week you can find help on your journey on the Blazing Glory website. But never forget that all the help you need is in your manual (Bible) and in your heart hideaway, and that your helper, Jesus, is just a prayer away.

If you do not already know God as your Father and Jesus as your friend, and you would like to, then why not go to your special hideaway and pray the following short prayer:

"Father, please forgive me for the times I have not been true to you and what you say. I am sorry for all the wrong things I have done, and from today I want to be free to live in your truth. I thank you, Jesus, that you paid the price for each one of my sins and I receive the forgiveness found at the cross. I receive you – the truth – into my life and I know that through you I now have eternal life. I pray that your Holy Spirit will live in me and guide me in your way. Amen."

Jesus has now come into your life and he promises never to leave you if you follow his ways. If you want to, you could tell a good friend, family member or adult whom you trust that you have just done this. Or you could tell the Blazing Glory team by sending an email to us at info@blazing-glory.com